3

All stories appear here for the first time, with the exception of 'Jacob Stanley', which was originally published in the January 2018 issue of Writing Magazine.

A WHISPER FROM ME TO YOU

TEN SHORT STORIES

ANDREW ALLEN

APRIL 2020

About the author

Andrew Allen lives in Brighton, East Sussex. His previous works include *Doctor Who: Loud And Proud* for Big Finish – Short Trips, *The Bone Merchant* and *The Slow Invasion* for Candy Jar Books' Lethbridge-Stewart series, and a series of plays, including *Year Without Summer*, about Mary Shelley's half sister Claire Clairmont, *Four Play*, a murder mystery farce with four actors each playing four parts (and with four different endings), and *One Woman Alien* – one woman, one hour, one classic horror movie.

@my_grayne

A WHISPER FROM ME TO YOU

A NOTE FROM THE AUTHOR

So, here are some stories.

Some have been hanging around for a while, waiting to be released into the wild. Some of them were started a couple of years ago, and only finished this year (2020). I think there's a fear deeply threaded into the DNA of many writers – I can't be the only one, surely – of actually finishing their work, and offering it up to public consumption. It's not all terror about the possibility that you might not be good enough: 'It's not failure you're scared of, a teacher once said to me in genuinely the only experience I ever had that could come even close to Inspirational Teacher Moment, 'it's fear of success – once people find out you're good at something, they'll want to know what else you've got.'

Some of the fear (a lot of it) is not even that clever. It's no more elegant a reason than shoddy discipline, and obviously a big deciding factor is when an author panics that their work is not good enough (a thread I'm not inclined to pull at too hard in an introduction to my own collection of short stories).

But some of is the danger of the SHINY NEW THING – the moment, inevitable in almost every writing project, when the hard work gets slightly too hard, and you get a new idea that's much more brilliant, much more fantastic, than whatever else it is you're working on. It can far too easily mean that you are constantly distracted.

That is of course, fatal to any writer – you run the very real risk of starting lots of BRILLIANT new stories, but never even finishing the mediocre ones. (I should acknowledge, by the way, that I'm selling myself slightly short here – I've finished *tons* of stories. Some of which, as you might have guessed, are contained within this very collection). I have certainly been guilty of getting distracted once or twice.

Maybe more than twice.

The point is, I've managed to stack up a good pile of shiny new things. And I'm probably a good while away from doing this writing thing full-time, right? So my stories – like most things that you and I do for our passion and pleasure when we're not putting in hours at whatever pays the bills – they get pushed to the side hours, the edges of life. Which is to say that I recently made a list of all the stories – short tales, novels, plays, whatever – that I have right here

(I'm pointing at my head now)

And I worked out that it's going to take me fifteen, twenty years to get all these things written, and out there. And that's not even including all the other shiny new things – the ideas I haven't had yet. So, I thought, I'd better get started at finishing, and avoid the risk of dying before I actually finish the damn things.

As far as themes go, these ten stories are a mixed bag, although like most story collections, I'm sure you can find a common thread running through them if you look hard enough. They involve a lonely little boy, a resentful vampire, an astronaut trapped in the machine that's supposed to preserve her life, a woman who isn't a werewolf, a deal with the devil, and the most powerful woman in the country accused of witchcraft.

Oh, and also a dirty weekend in Brighton.

I hope you find something to distract you.

ANDREW ALLEN
APRIL 2020

JACOB STANLEY

SCHOOL REUNION

CRITICAL MASS

PLENTY MORE PEBBLES

FREE

THE MAN WITH CLEAR GREY EYES

WHERE WOLF

A WHISPER FROM ME TO YOU

BROOM HANDLE

EVERY LITTLE THING SHE DOES

COMING SOON FROM ANDREW ALLEN

JACOB STANLEY

Jacob Stanley, who, at the age of just six, is not yet aware that his name is actually made up of two different first names, stands at the front of the bus, and drives. It's his favourite part of coming into town with his mum.

From his vantage point – front of the bus, right hand side – he can hold out his hands to hold an imaginary steering wheel (except to him, it's not imaginary, not at all) and steer the bus wherever he likes. He is vaguely aware that he is being watched by almost everybody else on the top deck. His travelling companions at this hour are usually small white haired women in heavy coats, scarves and gloves. They coo over him and remark on what a good boy he is. He and his mum take this journey three times a week, and many of the women's faces are familiar to him, even if he is too shy to respond when they speak to him.

As well as being six, he is small for his age, and this attracts a great deal of attention. Usually, it's the unwanted kind – bullying, that kind of thing – but recently, that has eased off slightly. Jacob knows that he is not completely invisible to the other kids at school, but they have started to treat him like he is. He prefers it this way, being allowed to move around undisturbed in his own little space. Much like now.

He knows that his mum is sitting about two seats behind him, watching carefully. This usually annoys him, but only a little. He knows that it would be easy for her to sit right next to him, not letting him out of her sight, her hand resting gently but firmly on his shoulder. He is, after all, only six. What he really wants, of course, is to be left alone to drive the bus on his own, to have his mum sitting on the bottom deck. But he knows why she keeps him in sight, and he is glad that she is there.

The bus swings violently to the left, and Jacob is momentarily confused before he remembers that it's Friday, and on Fridays the bus goes directly to the depot without going up the high street first. It's actually the reason they've come into town today – the farmer's market.

His mum gets some meat for Sunday's lunch, while Jacob hopes he'll get some chocolate from the ladies at the sweet stall. Apparently he has very big blue eyes. The second woman at the stall always tells him he'll be a heartbreaker when he's older.

He adjusts the mime of the steering wheel to accommodate the change of direction and looks, as he always does, at the cars coming up the road in the opposite direction. From where he's standing, it looks like each car is being swallowed up by the bus itself. He imagines the front of the bus being filled with teeth, devouring every car it sees. The image delights him at first, and then within a matter of seconds, horrifies him. He shakes his head as if the horrible pictures will fall away with every flick of his hair.

The bus pulls into the depot and comes to a stop. Everyone gathers their bags and begins to leave, chatting comfortably. His mum calls to him, and he takes a moment to reassure himself that the bus has indeed come to a full stop. He mimes taking his hands off the steering wheel, and joins his mum as they both climb down the stairs to the lower level of the bus. They are the last two to get off.

As he and his mum hop off the bus, his hand feels strangely empty, and he doesn't really know why. About a year ago (actually, it's only eight months, but to Jacob it feels much longer), he had begun to wrestle his hand impatiently out of his mum's whenever they crossed the road together. He had told her that he was a big boy now. She had protested, but not for long, seeming defeated. He suspected that he had upset her somehow, but he couldn't work out why. After all, it wasn't her feelings being hurt, but his – he just didn't want to be treated like a baby anymore.

Of course, that was at the beginning of the year, before the summer. Now, he finds that sometimes, he actually *wants* his mum to take his hand and in fact misses holding it as they cross the road. On a couple of occasions recently, he has held up his mittened hand to her gloved one – but she seems not to notice. He almost does this now, but as he steps off the bus, directly behind his mother, he stops, looking at his hand. There's nothing in it. For some reason, a reason he can't quite make sense of, this looks wrong, or at least unusual. He even pats himself, trying to work out what he's missing. If any of the other passengers looked over at him right now, he would look to them like a miniature version of an elderly gent who has misplaced his keys.

Jacob freezes, suddenly realising what it is he has forgotten. He leaps back onto the bus (the doors are still open, not that it has occurred to him that they might have shut) and he climbs the stairs with quiet determination.

Nobody notices his journey – the driver is writing something in a battered old file, and his mum has bumped into a friend just outside the bus, and has fallen into the same quiet conversation. These days, it's always the same quiet conversation. The friend asks how she is, a hand on her arm. His mum always gives the same answer, which is a lie. They ask if there is any news. She always gives them the same answer, which they already know. They offer to make a meal and bring it over. On this last point, this last promise, they never deliver.

Jacob doesn't hear any of this. He has realised what is missing from his hand, and he knows where to go to find it again. The doll is exactly where he left her, on the front seat of the bus. She sat watching while he drove. He stole it from his sister's bedroom last week, although he isn't precisely sure that 'stolen' is the correct word, all things considered. Ever since his sister was born, he has been told how lucky he is to have his own bedroom. He supposes this is true, although in the last couple of weeks, he has woken in the middle of the night, and felt unable to sleep until he creeps into his sister's bedroom. He never sleeps in his sister's bed, of course. Sleeping on the floor is enough. He wakes up again early each morning and goes back to his own bedroom. It never occurs to him to wonder if his mum knows what he's doing. She probably does.

The doll is not his sister's favourite. She prefers the more lifelike one, with hair you can brush. He hasn't taken that one, he thinks that maybe his sister would shout at him if she ever caught him touching it. Recently, he has begun to think that would be a pretty good reason to take the more lifelike doll – he doesn't think he would mind being shouted at by his sister. But for now, he has taken this doll instead, which he seems to remember is called a ragdoll. He doesn't know why, because it seems to be all straight lines – no ragged edges at all.

He took it because it looks – a little – like his sister. Not completely, of course: his sister, like Jacob himself, has very blonde hair, and this doll's hair is the colour of rust. But the length of the hair is about the same – it hits the shoulders – and more importantly, the doll wears a dress that looks almost exactly like the one his sister wore almost every day this summer. It has blue stripes crossing over one another, creating little white squares between them. Where each blue stripe crosses over another, it darkens to a much smaller square, a slightly darker blue. Jacob will sometimes stare at these dark blue squares for ages, hoping to see something hidden there. Something everybody else has missed.

'JACOB!'

His mother's voice slams into his day-dreaming like a slap. She's standing at the top of the stairs, swaying slightly, and she looks like she has been crying. Jacob is completely confused; he has lost all sense of where he is. He holds the doll up to his mum, thinking that it might explain everything. It appears to make everything worse, because his mum's face crumples into uncontrollable sobs. At first, this scares Jacob, and then, when it appears that nothing bad is going to happen, he begins to cry as well, still clutching the doll that reminds him of his sister. His mum comes over to him very quickly. She is there so suddenly that Jacob thinks she must have run to him, but she has always told him not to run on the bus. He thinks for a moment that she is angry, and that she is about to take the doll back, ripping it out of his hands. This somehow scares him more than her crying and he grips onto the doll even more tightly. His mum doesn't take the doll back. She simply drops to her knees and wraps her arms around him, doll and all. Her tears wet his cheeks, which are already clammy with his own tears.

She holds him very tight, and says the same words over and over again, but unable to finish whatever sentence she is trying to say. 'I thought .. I thought ..' She breathes in his hair. Jacob thinks that perhaps he might say his sister's name. That would be nice. Nobody has said his sister's name out loud in a very long time.

SCHOOL REUNION

Stephen pushed the door open, wincing. He had walked around the block twice already, and he felt that was as much as could reasonably be expected of him today, despite the fact that it was only – he checked his watch – quarter to six. He was waking up earlier and earlier these days. He tried to stay in bed for as long as possible now, knowing that the day would be intolerably long, but even as early as four, it felt like his every joint had stiffened into a rock hard, seemingly immovable position. By the time he eventually got up – and then only because he couldn't bear the pain any longer – his entire body was slicked in grimy sweat.

It always took him at least half an hour of grim determination and effort to simply get himself into a position where he was sitting on the edge of the bed, both feet planted on the bedroom floor. This action alone had him breathing hard, head swimming. Eighty nine years old, and the body that had served him so well for the best part of a century was betraying him. No, not just betraying him; it was punishing him – it didn't even have the decency to abandon him and let him die, as had happened with so many of his friends. It wouldn't be as bad (he told himself) if everything was just shutting down, if he found one day that he actually couldn't walk at all, but things weren't as straightforward as that - everything still worked, to a fashion. But not as consistently as it had back when he could rely on it unthinkingly as a kid, and always laced through with that pain. He had put a lot of work into this body over the years, and now it chose to repay him by not being in any way reliable.

Now, he had to do even the most basic things through gritted teeth. He wasn't stupid, of course you expected that kind of thing to kick in by the time you got to ninety (or one year shy of ninety, let's not age ourselves out of the market just yet): he didn't think that he would be able to put in the kind of days that he had when he was twenty. But expecting old age to come over the horizon was quite a different thing to walking along, minding your own business, and finding that you had walked into the neighbourhood of the horizon all by yourself.

Now that he *was* that age, he didn't quite know how to cope: if he had begun to be frail, if his limbs had started to shake, if his eyes had failed him – if any of these things had happened – well, he would have been as pissed off as he was now, that much was in his nature – but at least it would have made some kind of *sense* to him. But this? This hell, when his muscles suggested that he could still lift a piano with one hand without breaking a sweat, but just walking or breathing – the mere acting of *existing* – apparently that was too much to cope with. This, Stephen thought, was the ultimate proof of God's existence, if only to state that God was a being of exceptional cruelty.

But despite all of this, he did not – apparently – qualify for any home help. It wasn't as if he was too proud to ask for it: in fact, he had been surprised – frankly astounded – when he was told that, in the opinion of the local health authority, it was considered that he was fully able to clean his apartment – and indeed himself – without any assistance. He was eighty nine, for Chrissake. He didn't doubt that there were weaker individuals than he – he had taken very good care of himself over the years, after all – but what was the point of being healthy all of his life if, just when he was beginning to ask for help for the very first time, he was beaten to the punch by some greedy fat slob who had smoked all his life?

He had tried telling the maddeningly impassive girl at the office about all the times he had spent crawling – literally, crawling – up the staircase to his apartment, felled by the pain when he was only halfway through his journey. He had told her about the countless times he had been trapped in his own bath, joints locking, the water cooling to ice around him. But of course, the only days he could get to the office to tell them all of this was on comparatively good days. His very presence there made his words a lie. They never believed that his situation was quite as difficult as he told them it was.

Although, that wasn't quite true, was it? They knew he was telling the truth. He could see it in their eyes, in their hooded look, the way they avoided looking directly back at him, the way their lips pursed as they tap-tapped his answers to their formulaic questions on their computers. It would surely be better for them all if he just did the decent thing and died; it would probably save a few dollars and cents from the welfare state, and he had no doubt that once everybody his apartment block was gone, the entire place could be sold on by the local landlords for a pretty decent profit.

He winced again. Already the bitter tang of bile was filling his mouth. This morning, he had ridden down in the lift, marvelling that for once it was working (the dull stench of urine had remained, so pervasive seemed like it had somehow soaked into the metal of the lift walls themselves). It had been too much, he supposed, to expect that the lift would still be working by the time he got back, and so it proved to be: when he jabbed a finger on the button, there was the familiar taunting sound of clanging metal, followed by – nothing.

The lift had been repaired just last Monday, and in this block of flats, it seemed the kids could never let a full week go by without breaking it again. He had no doubt whatsoever that it *was* the kids who kept on vandalising the lift, despite never actually seeing them do it. He had certainly heard them though, late at night, laughing and screaming at one another. He supposed that none of them gave a damn about the old man who lived on the top floor, whose once powerful legs were now so weak it could take him the best part of an hour to climb four flights of stairs.

He muttered to himself (he was never sure *what* he muttered to himself, he never articulated any words, but muttering incoherent nonsense was what he did in order to stop himself from sighing all the time) and gripped the bannister to pull himself upwards. Sharp pain ripped into his calves with each upward step, making him want to weep. He never cried, however. If life (and his own father, dead now for over fifty years) had taught him anything, it was that you got what you wanted and needed a lot more easily if you kept your cards to your chest and your emotions firmly in place. Stephen had lived his nearly ninety years without ever feeling the need to look up the meaning of the word *cliché*, and would have comfortably denied the accusation if it had ever been levelled at him: it wasn't a cliché, but a fact; hard and immovable - Grown Men Do Not Cry.

He stopped. He was halfway up, and he needed to take a breather. His knuckles were bone white as he gripped the bannister. His vision became milky, it felt like there was cotton wool trapped in his skull, and he muttered to himself again to keep the world in focus. He did this for nearly five minutes, steeling himself for the rest of the journey. This was not going to be easy. And of course, now he had news to carry on his shoulders.

The doctor had told him in an emotionless, no-nonsense way. Stephen had demanded that much. In fact, he had demanded as much back in 1955, when he had first met the man who was to be his lifelong doctor for the very first time. Back when he was young. Fit and immortal. No need to screw around with fancy words and dishonest hedging. Not in the doctor's office. Nowadays, Doctor Faraday knew Stephen well, and knew not to sugar-coat. Stephen had waited long enough for the test results to come through; when Doctor Faraday had invited him in for 'a chat', Stephen knew that the news was not going to be good.

'So what do we have – months?'

Doctor Faraday had managed to get halfway through his routine answer – that it was very difficult to estimate in these circumstances, that each individual case was entirely different – before clamping his mouth shut, taking a deep breath, and fixing Stephen with a reproachful glance. 'You really should have come to me much sooner. The cancer is very aggressive. It's far too late to operate.'

Stephen said nothing, simply returning the his gaze, waiting for him to answer the question, the only question that actually mattered. Eventually, his doctor sighed. 'I'm not convinced that we can be talking about 'months', plural,' he said at last. 'It could be anytime.' Another pause followed then, both men wondering in the silence if Stephen would simply drop dead there and then in the office.

He walked on. Upwards. Only now did it occur to him that he should have asked if the pain he was having to endure was directly or even tangentially associated with the cancer, but he supposed that was a question that could wait until next time, if he managed to stay around until a next time. Certainly he had never received a decent answer when he demanded to know what pain relief was available to stop him screaming in the middle of the night. Right now, he just wanted to get back to his apartment. He thought he had just about enough energy to get to his door, and then collapse back on his bed.

Back in the day, nobody would ever dare mess with him – he had been the biggest man around. Not exactly tall, but that didn't matter. He had always looked after himself, but now what had once been tightly packed muscle was disappearing into gristle and strained sinew. The speed at which this was happening was alarming.

He supposed it was the fault of the cancer that he hadn't bothered to get checked until it was too late. It was, he thought, a good thing that he would be dead soon: the pain he endured every day was so furious it felt like a sentient punishment. He reflected that he hadn't really needed a doctor to tell him about the cancer: the three extra holes he'd had to punch into his belt had all been the postcards he'd needed.

There was, he thought, a cruel irony in getting this far – *nearly ninety*, he reminded himself – and still getting one last scare from cancer. He was supposed to die in his sleep (which he might still do, he acknowledged), but this was just mean. He had struggled to come up with a concept for what it made him feel like, and the best he could think of was clumsy, but apt enough: it was like dropping what would have been your last scoop of ice-cream just as you were preparing to savour every last taste – it wasn't as if anyone was going to have that much sympathy with you – you'd already had the rest of it, after all – but still, the pleasant, delicious ending that you'd promised yourself was stolen from you at the very last moment.

Stephen stopped, his breath – already hitching due to the exertion of climbing the stairs - dying away in his throat. There was a figure standing in his doorway. He had heard of people being mugged outside their very own door before, but until now nobody had tried it with him. His hands balled into fists. The man standing in the doorway was taller than Stephen, but somehow managed to look smaller at the same time. Perhaps it was his slight frame. He did look like he was a lot thinner – scrawny, in fact. Or perhaps it was to do with the pale, pinched expression on the young man's face. Stephen did not break stride as he walked towards his door. As decrepit as he was, he could still pack a punch. If this kid wanted trouble, he would find that just one swipe of the fist from this old man would settle most arguments very easily. Sure, Stephen would then have to put up with an extra bout of pain in his shoulder for a week or two, but this kid wouldn't know that. All this kid would know for sure would be his brand new busted lip.

'Help you?' Stephen muttered shortly in a tone designed to convey that no help whatsoever was being offered. He had already produced his keys. The young man stepped to one side as Stephen reached his door. He was vaguely aware of the smell of aftershave. A good smell. Expensive. The sort of smell young men put on when they're out on the town. Looking for companionship. Stephen breathed in heavily for a moment. It had been a very long time since he himself had been out on the town. A long time since he had met an unaccompanied woman at a bar. There had been a time when a woman on her own had always accepted your offer of a drink, no matter what you looked like or what you did. No longer. Either the woman wanted more, or he had become less. Either way, those days were long gone. Maybe twenty – no, *fifty* – years ago. Was that even possible?

The young man smiled. A salesman's smile. Stephen's eyes were not as good as they used to be, but still, he rarely missed a trick. The young man's smile was false, a mask.

He spoke. 'You don't recognise me.' It was a statement, not a question, and spoken with no expectation of an answer. In fact, it sounded like a declaration of Stephen's weakness – of his failure. That he was *supposed* to know who this young man was. He was right, though: Stephen didn't recognise him at all. The only people he saw these days were either as old as he was, or the kids in scrubs sticking needles into his arms. This boy was neither. He seemed quite excited though, his eyes sparkling in the gloom as he looked Stephen up and down. He licked his lips, suddenly pulling out an asthma inhaler, sucking on it violently.

Stephen swayed on his feet slightly, nonplussed by what had just happened – or rather, what hadn't. A young man was standing outside the door of his apartment – blocking Stephen's way to his own home, in fact – and had suddenly, and without warning, pulled something out of his coat pocket. Sure, it had only been his inhaler, and not a knife, or a gun, but Stephen hadn't known that, at least not at first. And what had Stephen done in response? Absolutely nothing. No reaction whatsoever. If this boy's intention *had* been to mug him, or to kill him, then he would have succeeded, and done so easily. Stephen's reaction time had apparently slowed to a fatal crawl. He felt old. Even older than his nearly ninety years. Worse than that, he felt stupid.

He brought the key up to the lock, and faltered, realising that if he opened the door, there was at least the outside chance that this young man could push past him and into his apartment. He could simply rip the key out of his hand right now, come to that.

'I don't have anything worth stealing,' he said, 'and I don't care if you don't believe me.' With that, he opened the door, and walked in. The young man held onto the door before Stephen could close it behind him. He looked at the young man with astonishment that almost immediately fell away to fury. The young man simply looked at him with an infuriatingly bland smile.

'I'm Peter,' the younger man said, and then said nothing more. His tone was light and calm, but also firm. It seemed that 'Peter' was not going to elaborate on his identity. At least, not yet. There was, Stephen realised, a mild tone of expectation in his voice, and it was clear that Peter still expected Stephen to recognise him somehow, a superior kind of attitude that was slightly undermined by the kid once again sucking on his inhaler. Stephen was already beginning to get irritated by this tender slip of a boy, with his constant flipping back of his golden hair, who was apparently unable to get through a single sentence without chugging back on his inhaler every few –

Stephen swallowed. *The inhaler. Peter.*

'You're dead,' Stephen said, finally. His voice pitched higher than he would have liked. Peter shrugged, and smiled. 'I suppose that's technically true,' he said. He tapped on Stephen's door, using the hand that was gripping the inhaler. 'Got time for a chat? Something I need to talk to you about.' Stephen was already shaking his head – almost in instinct – when Peter continued, with a little more steel in his voice. 'I think you owe me that much, at least. Since it was you that got me killed.'

*

Stephen walked around his own apartment in not much more than a daze. If he had been thinking clearly in any way, he would no doubt have marvelled at how quickly someone can accept – and adapt to – a reality they would have previously considered impossible. You have to, really. The only other option was to surrender to insanity, and Stephen wasn't quite ready to do that yet. Death, he was already on nodding terms with. Crazy could wait.

Eventually, he sat down on the edge of the bed, and looked up at the kid who was calling himself Peter, who was leaning against the wall, watching Stephen with an infuriatingly patient air. 'How old are you?

Stephen asked suddenly. It was a stupid question, but somehow the only one that made sense right now. If he decided to believe what Peter was telling him (and despite himself, he was beginning to do exactly that), then it was obvious how old Peter was, just as it was obvious that there were two completely different answers to that single question, and that both answers contradicted one another just as much as not.

If Peter was indeed Peter, then he was the same age as Stephen: they had been in the same class at school, and their birthdays had been within weeks of one another. If Stephen was eighty-nine, then Peter was, too. Time did not stand still for your friends when they were out of your sight, no matter how much it felt like it did. Except that Peter had never been a friend, and it looked like for him, time had stood very still indeed.

Which meant – again, if this man claiming to be Peter was telling the truth – that the other, contradictory thing was true – that he was just thirteen, because he was completely unchanged since Stephen had last saw him, when he had gone missing.

Thirteen. Just a kid. Back in those days, being just thirteen actually *meant* being just thirteen. Now, the average teen knew about sex (and drugs, and whatever had replaced rock n' roll these days) much more than Stephen himself had known at that age (no matter what he would have attempted to claim at the time). But back when Peter had been thirteen, he had really just been a child, a slight, fragile looking boy. It had made him an easy target for bullies like Stephen (he was under no illusion about what he had been when he was younger: he had been a bully. He wasn't stupid, and it was impossible – futile, even – to define, or even defend his behaviour as anything other than bullying. Stephen had never felt any shame or regret about this. In fact, if anything, he had always been slightly irritated at so-called 'victims' like Peter: it was their fault, drawing attention to themselves.

Peter, standing before him now, was the same slight and fragile child Stephen remembered from almost seven decades before. But now, looking at him from the perspective of an adult, Stephen saw something that had previously been invisible to him: the fragility lent Peter an undeniable beauty that almost radiated from him, blonde hair catching in the light, eyelashes that were almost feminine. Exactly the kind of things that had encouraged (forced, really) Stephen and his friends to beat the shit out of Peter when they were kids. Now, he could see that they were also the sort of qualities that might ultimately lead some sex pest to abduct him.

That had been the story that had sprung up in the weeks and months around Peter's disappearance. Stephen couldn't remember where he had heard it first: the gleefully gruesome rumours of murder that circulated around school, or the oddly coy warnings from his parents. Whenever the stories were shared, they were almost always distilled to a single phrase: *dirtyoldman*.

It had taken a few days for the neighbourhood to truly comprehend the seriousness of what had happened – kids were always running away from home, or hitching a ride to the one bar at the edge of town, or going on fishing trips and not feeling any urgent need to return home. So when Peter's mother had begun to raise the alarm, her concerns were initially ignored, perhaps not realising that while her family was just as impoverished as anyone else's, she and her son actually got on in a way that many families did not (another reason why Peter attracted the attention of bullies), and that his disappearance truly was out of character. By the time the police started to show an interest, nobody expected to see Peter again alive.

None of which really explained why Peter was now standing in his apartment, unchanged for the better part of seventy years. Stephen's mind had already desperately tried to come up with some attempt at logic: that this was not Peter at all, but some relative – a grandson or distant cousin for instance, who had somehow discovered the link between he and Stephen and was now seeking to exploit the situation, perhaps in an attempt to exact revenge for the bullying, or maybe to extort money from Stephen.

But logic was no help here: Stephen knew, he absolutely *knew* that this boy was the kid who had gone missing decades before. It didn't matter that such a thing should have been impossible, now that he could see Peter right in front of him, Stephen found it remarkably easy to accept the insane truth. He supposed it explained why Peter's body had never been found – it had never been buried or even dumped in a shallow grave – it was here, walking around in Stephen's apartment, wearing a face that wore a shit-eating grin, and all the time sucking on that inhaler.

'What happened to you?' Stephen asked, and as soon as he had done so, it felt remarkable that he had taken so long. Maybe seeing a ghost will do that to you, Stephen thought, and then on top of that: *is he a ghost? Why didn't he just walk through your door? Why did he wait to ask permission to come in?* He realised he wasn't listening to Peter's answer, and forced himself to focus.

'So I took to taking the long way home,' Peter was saying. 'I don't know if you guys knew about that, or if you cared. I just knew that if I walked my normal route home, you'd be waiting for me.'

Stephen considered arguing the point: he and his friends had always sat on the wall outside the grocery store for no better reason than it was there. Certainly not because they were lying in wait for Peter to go past. But it was also true that they would have found it impossible to let him walk past them without a few kicks and punches. Stephen dimly remembered someone in the gang declaring that if Peter didn't want to draw attention to himself, then he should go another way. Perhaps that someone had been Stephen himself. He could no longer remember; it had been so long ago. If Peter had heard the advice or not was unimportant – he had started to walk home another way, across the wasteland, which had been a rather grand name for a football pitch sized stretch of land behind a row of houses where there was no street lighting.

It had been on the wasteland where Peter had been taken.

Peter smiled. He seemed almost wistful. 'There was a fifty yard clearing around me in all directions. I never saw him coming. Although I did hear a flapping of wings, so I'm guessing he ...' at this, Peter pointed upward, and dropped his hand to slap his own neck. Involuntarily, Stephen followed the direction of his hand, and looked up also. When he looked down again, he found that Peter was looking at him, waiting. 'Although I might have embellished that while I was recovering. All I know is that I've never again seen a vampire who can turn into a bat.' Stephen stared at Peter, waiting for a punchline that was not forthcoming. He desperately wanted to confirm the point – *did you just tell me that you got attacked by a vampire?* – but found that he could not speak. The words, ironically, stuck in his throat.

Peter seemed to lose interest in him, and walked over to the window, pulling back the frayed curtain and peering out at the traffic below. There was a ringing in Stephen's ears, and the word *vampire* bounced around in his skull a few times, waiting for him to make sense of it.

Finally, he came up for air, like a man who has been drowning. 'You're not a vampire,' he said. 'Don't fuck me around.'

Peter, still looking out of the window, gave a polite nod, and

He was at Stephen's side. The distance between the window and the bed on which Stephen sat was at least ten metres, but Peter had got there in less time than it would have taken Stephen to blink, once. He was there so immediately that Stephen was certain he could feel the air being pushed out of the way to accommodate the sudden arrival of his body. Peter snarled at Stephen's neck, pointed teeth protruding from his mouth. 'Don't tell me what I am, and what I'm not,' Peter hissed. It was the first time he had sounded anything other than completely calm. Stephen didn't answer; his heart pounding in his chest, something that up until now had only been a concept before; now it felt like his heart was desperate to splinter his ribcage in an effort to escape.

'Vampires exist,' Peter said, 'and I'm one of them.' He smiled, and Stephen noticed that the pointed teeth had vanished. He wondered briefly – hopefully – if they had been fake – perhaps Peter had stuck them in when he had been facing away from Stephen at the window – but he reluctantly rejected the idea. The pace at which Peter had sped across the room was impossible to deny.

'Let's go through the basics, shall we?' Peter suggested, and he seemed to be enjoying himself. He was a lot more confident than he was when he had been thirteen (thirteen the first time round), Stephen reflected. Maybe being dead will do that for you.

'Yes, I drink blood. No, I don't need to drink blood to stay alive.' He stopped, and smirked. 'Let's just say "alive" for the sake of argument, shall we? Makes things easier. I can't be killed.' The smirk vanished. 'Believe me, I've tried. I don't need blood to stay alive, but if I don't drink blood, I get very sick. Best to keep to the diet, I've found.'

He walked around the room, ticking off further points by tapping one finger to another. 'I can walk around in sunlight, although it gives me a massive migraine.' He glanced at Peter, giving him a wide smile. 'I recommend some kind of hat. Stake to the heart, crosses..' he shrugged. 'No effect whatsoever.' He threw out his arms, in a gesture that perversely reminded Stephen of the crucifix that had hung in their classroom all those years ago. 'I'm undead, and I'm going to be around for until the end of time, perhaps even longer.' He dropped his arms. 'So far, it's been a lot better than when I was alive.'

He pulled out the plastic tube and gulped on it again. A frantic *shuck* sound. A question began to occur to Stephen, but before he could give it full voice, Peter answered his burgeoning query. 'Ain't it cruel?' he remarked, with a smile so embittered it actually made him beautiful. 'I don't even have to breathe anymore, and I still got the asthma.' That old Brooklyn twang. 'I've met vampires that had the 'flu when they were taken, or even just a cough.' He smirked again. 'That's the worst, that's the meanest – to have a body that's got a cough, and *that's* what gets preserved for eternity.' His smile widened, and once again, he looked beautiful. 'I had it lucky,' Peter suggested. 'I only had asthma when I was taken. There are those who have it a lot worse.' He stopped, lost in thought. He seemed to come to some kind of internal decision, and pocketed the inhaler. He turned to face Stephen properly, simply fixing him with a stare that gave nothing away. It seemed to Stephen that there were flecks of gold in Peter's eyes. It was the one thing about his face that looked genuinely supernatural.

'Why did you come here, Peter?' he demanded at last. His voice shook, and he found that he didn't care.

Peter smiled – *I thought you'd never ask,* the expression suggested – and said in a pleasant tone that did not sound pleasant at all, 'I came to visit you, Stephen.' He fixed Stephen with an unblinking stare, a stare that Stephen, to his immense irritation, found that he could not match. 'I thought about coming to see you years ago, back when we were still kids.' He made a play of inspecting his fingernails, but Stephen was certain there was no need; Peter's nails looked immaculate, and he surely didn't need to check. 'Back when *you* were a kid,' Peter clarified.

Peter chuckled at that and sat down next to Stephen again, but this time did not do it at speed; clearly he considered that he had all the time in the world. 'I waited til now,' he said, and dropped his head on

Stephen's shoulder, his mouth at Stephen's neck. Stephen could feel Peter smile, and began to pull away. 'Now seemed like the right time,' Peter continued, and took Stephen's hand, like a hopeful youngster toward the end of a date.

'This is the way it works,' Peter explained. A vampire chooses you. They feed. If they wish you to join, they will make you feed on them.'

Stephen didn't answer. He was still trying to pull his neck away from Peter's mouth – *dear God could he feel teeth?* – and tried to take his hand out of Peter's seemingly relaxed grip, and found that he couldn't. Stephen started to panic. It was no use.

'The first time I drank, I vomited.'

'Peter – please.'

Peter drew away for a moment, once again looking at Stephen with fascination.

With hunger.

He smiled. His smile was beautiful.

His grip became even tighter. Stephen swung his other hand around, attempting to peel Peter's fingers away. It was no use. Peter continued speaking, undisturbed and nonchalant.

'My sire forced me to taste his blood, again and again. It didn't take too long before I drank my fill.'

Inspiration came to Stephen, brilliant and true.

'I – I've got cancer. I've got cancer. You don't want my blood.'

The gold in Peter's eyes shone. He gave a sad little pout – *oh, bless you* – and nuzzled back at Stephen's neck. 'I shouldn't worry about that. I'm not asking for a donation.'

Peter opened his mouth. A sigh. Wetness at Stephen's throat. A low chuckle. Peter clamped his mouth down. Stephen tried to call out, but couldn't. He could hear the sound of lips smacking, of something that sounded disgustingly like milkshake being sucked through a straw. The world went grey, then yellow, and then – after it felt like all the moisture had been bleached from his eyeballs – there was only white.

*

There was the sound of shredding. He still could not see. He could feel Peter grab him by the back of the head, and force him forward. He didn't need to see to know that his mouth was being pushed onto an open, ragged wound. By the time he was able to start screaming, his mouth was full of blood.

He began to drink. Anything to make it stop.

*

It took him three hours. He had to stop and start several times. He even had to stop to catch his breath, even though he was fairly certain he wasn't breathing anymore. But he didn't vomit, not once. Peter told him he was very proud.

*

Sunlight streamed through the window. Stephen was already wincing in pain before he was truly awake. He could tell straight away that he was on the floor, and wondered how long it would take for him to get to even the recovery position, let alone kneeling. He brought up his fingers to touch the wound on his throat, and hissed. Still tender. Hopefully that would heal up before too long. He dropped his hand, and let his head hang back. He could see the apartment door still open: Peter had not closed it on his way out after having given Stephen his gift. The shaft of sunlight danced on Stephen's forehead, just above the eyebrows. Peter had told the truth: the sun did result in an immediate migraine. He would move soon, as soon as he was able to find the energy. But in the meantime, the migraine was a different sort of pain than all the others he usually had to endure.

He thought about Peter, wherever Peter was now, taken by a vampire when he was young and had a bad bout of asthma, and smiled. Asthma? Some people had it so easy.

When a kid from the floor below found him eleven hours later, Stephen was ready to feed. Took his mind off the pain.

CRITICAL MASS

The first thing that General Amelia Lane knew for sure was that everyone else on the ship was either dead, or at least in as much trouble as she herself was. Mentally, she grappled toward her training in an effort to repel her every instinct that would doubtless cause her to make the wrong decision, or even to panic. Not that she was by nature a person prone to panic; but on the other hand, falling to a certain death was the sort of experience likely to make one pick up all sorts of bad habits.

For now, she had to let the ship look after her – or at least, the last part of the ship that apparently survived. Less than four minutes ago, the computer had pumped the appropriate chemicals and adrenalin into her system to violently rip her out of hypersleep, and had immediately flooded her body with a whole cocktail of other drugs to ensure that the sudden shock didn't kill her, and that she could be alert and responsive within seconds.

It was quite a switch, flipping from coma to fully alert in less time than it took to take a single breath, but throughout her training she had always been assured that once she was awake, it would feel like she had never been unconscious, and that she would be able to react – and act – immediately. It appeared that in this at least, everything that she had been told was correct. The digital readouts flashed before her eyes, giving her all the information she needed on the shield of reinforced industrial glass that served both as the pod's windscreen and her computer screen. Each of the sleep chambers – including the one that Amelia was in - had been rebooted to serve their secondary purpose as escape pods, and Amelia was now hurtling towards an unknown planet some few hundred miles below, on which she had so little detail it was simply named on her display as 'Unregistered Planet' – not even a suggestion of a Serial Code.

She looked at the readout once more, seeing no new information that contradicted what she'd already been led to understand: as far as she could ascertain, her pod was the only one that had been jettisoned. Either her crewmates were trapped in pods that could not escape the ship, or she had been flung to the planet due to some kind of mechanical fault, far away from the only people who could help her.

Amelia threw up a silent question (the pod was the same as the mothership, and could cope with basic mental enquires as long as your brainwaves were directly linked with the computer). The computer mused on her question for a little while, and then told her it didn't have an answer: the five other pods were MIA.

There was a short pause, and then the computer asked a question all of its own, requiring data so that it could answer a discrepancy that it could make no sense of: if General Lane was awake, then how (and why) were the pod's suspended animation facilities still in operation? For that, General Lane had no answer: she was still disturbed that the computer had not been able to contact any of the other pods. There was a very good chance that she was the last survivor of her crew. For the next few minutes, there was nothing she could do but wait for her enforced landing: her limbs were strapped in place, and she had learned all she could from the display.

*

Pod Three fell screaming out of the sky onto Unregistered Planet just before dawn. Dawn, that is, as an entirely abstract concept – Amelia had read no data to suggest that there were any existing lifeforms living on this planet who would have come up with any idea as complex and as suffocating as the concept of time. The pod slammed into the ground, which was soft enough not to offer too much resistance, but still – even within the safe confines of the pod itself – felt bone jarring. Amelia could see from her vantage point that the pod had managed to bury itself some way into the yielding earth. She waited a moment, and then spoke (*thought*) to the computer again. There was once more a moment's pause in which there was no answer, during which she began to wonder if the distance between the pod and the ship's main computer was too vast, or – worse – if the ship itself was no more. Finally, the computer informed her that she had survived the crash intact, no bones broken.

She unbuckled her supports that wrapped around her upper torso and arms, and allowed her body to hang forward slightly. She didn't have to ask the computer how much air she had, that was one of the pieces of information that she had on screen. The levels were comfortably in amber, which wasn't great, but not nearly as urgent as she had feared.

She estimated that she probably had about six days of oxygen within the pod now that it was separated from the main ship. She peered at the screen again, looking for assurance that she would be able to survive comfortably on the rock she now found herself on. It took a while for the pod's computer to call up the information (Amelia had the odd impression that the computer was distracted, and she wondered – not for the first time – if it was at least slightly sentient). Eventually, Amelia had the information she needed: this planet was comparable to Earth, at least in all the factors that were of immediate importance. She pressed her hand to release the dome of the pod so that she could climb out. The computer gave her a beep, a burble, and another beep.

And then nothing: the dome did not move.

It looked like the pod would require a more manual approach to allow her to get out of the damn thing. She looked up out of the window again, irritated that she could not get any sense of local time: something was wrong with the visuals, an almost strobing effect that flipped everything outside to *white black white black white black* so rapidly it was beginning to give her a headache. She considered unfastening the belt around her waist, but the pod had landed in a perfectly upright position, meaning that the belt was the only thing keeping her in place and preventing her from falling to the base of the pod, where she would have very little chance of making her escape.

Not, she thought bitterly to herself, that she had much of a chance anyway. The pod was perfectly sealed (why shouldn't it be; it's usual job was to be nothing other than a sleep pod for months at a time), and designed to pop open and expel its occupant upon landing as long as the immediate surroundings were safe. Which, according to the readout, they were.

So why was she still stuck in here?

black white black white black white black

Her fingers grazed over the keyboard, and stopped. Suddenly, her throat seemed far too tight. The information on the screen was wrong. It had to be wrong. She couldn't have come this far, avoided death on the mothership, avoided death again as the escape pod was flung out into deep space, and avoided death once more as she crashed onto this planet, only to be killed by the very thing that was supposed to protect her. She looked at the readout again, willing the information to change. The information stubbornly refused to alter.

The sealant on the nuclear chamber had a crack. There was enough power attached to the pod to keep a sleeping occupant alive for twenty years if needed, but there was also enough power to kill that person outright if there was any kind of accident. Which, it now appeared, there had been.

The crack was infinitesimally small at the moment, but the one thing that was undeniable about nuclear energy was that any kind of crack in the containment was by definition a crack too far. Even if Amelia managed to get out of this pod, she couldn't see that it would be possible to get clear of the blast in time to save her skin. She slumped, letting the back of her head gently hit the neck support. The information on the display repeated itself, a red line sent to mock her: just hours ago, her body had been flooded with chemicals in order to jolt her into wakefulness. Now, the pod she was trapped in was being flooded with a force that would pulverise the life from her.

white black white

The computer spoke to her, but this time it was not the voice in her head. Now, it was the image of a door, and a second image of a padlock clicking pleasingly into place. These two images were entirely separate, but were entirely equal. It would in fact not be accurate to describe them as images: they were ideas, concepts. But it was helpful for Amelia to solidify them as two separate images, to have a look at them and try to work out exactly what it was the computer was trying to tell her. Finally, it came to her, and when it did, it felt like the answer had always been there, waiting for her to discover it. Like buried treasure. *The door is closed. The door is locked.*

Amelia had nobody to widen her eyes at, but she widened them anyway: the pod had locked her in, and it wasn't going to let her out. Amelia tried to ask the computer what the hell it thought it was playing at, but she couldn't quite manage it: the words got in the way, and in any case, she wasn't quite sure what she was trying to ask. She looked at the images again. The padlock clicking into place was straightforward enough, but the door closing seemed oddly inverted. Back home, her wife had always complained that the world seemed made only for right-handed people, and now, stuck in this pod, looking at the image of a closing door that only existed in her subconscious, Amelia began to have some vague notion of what that probably felt like. The image of the closing door (*inverted*) seemed wrong somehow, like she was looking at it from the wrong angle, even as she stared at it more intently, and even as – as it swung shut – it blocked out that hateful flickering strobe effect: *black white black white black*. Once the door in her mind shut, it all became black, as if the door had shut out the sun.

The realisation slid into place with an almost audible click. *Like a padlock*, she thought. The door was closing her in, on the inside. The pod was protecting her. Protecting her from the strobe. She looked at the readout again. The orange light to signify the operation of suspended animation had not dimmed, and now the reason was painfully, laughably obvious: she was still in suspended animation. She was conscious, she was awake, she was able to move – but time *inside* the pod was moving at a different pace to anything *outside* the pod. She blinked a couple of times at the strobing, looking at it snap back and forth – *black white black white black white black white*. She was staring for nearly a full five minutes before she was able to comprehend – much less accept – that what she looking at was the passing of entire days and nights cycling over and over.

She calculated that it had been just over an hour since the pod had crashed. She looked at the days cycling over and over. Less than a second per cycle. That meant – that probably meant – that in the time since she had arrived, this planet had already passed through the equivalent of nearly ten years. The longest she had ever been suspended animation before was three months. If the pod didn't release her soon, it would be far too late for her to see anyone she loved ever again: for the time it would take for a day to pass in her perception, outside the pod it would be over 200 years. And as far as she could tell, there was nothing she could do. She leaned back and sighed. The pod did nothing. The days cycled on.

black white black white black white

She awoke. The things that had gathered outside the pod looked up, and waited. She slept.

She –

The things?

She awoke.

There were about a thousand of them, although from her angle it was difficult to be sure. Certainly it was hard to tell where their bodies ended or begun. They had the vague appearance of beetles, although not as hard-bodied. They were constantly moving, crawling over one another, in a swirling, writhing mass of bottle-green bodies. No matter the direction they crawled in however, their eyes were always on the pod.

On *her*.

She strained to look around, at any point on the horizon. If there was insect life here, then it was at least possible – not guaranteed, but possible – that there was other life here, someone that could help her. Help her before the pod reached baseline. She spoke to *(thought)* the computer again.

Find help.

The insects stopped.
The days and nights cycled on.

black white black white black

The insects watched.
She slept.

We serve.

The days and nights cycled on.

She awoke.

The insects – they weren't quite insects; they stood upright and their upper limbs looked more like regular, humanoid arms – were humming. It sounded like humming. Or singing.

We serve.

She thought that she was perhaps hallucinating. The humming (*singing*) was constant. The days and nights cycled on. The insects (*they're not insects*) bowed to her.

We serve.

She blinked, cursing her stupidity, her naivety. It must have been the shock of the crash. Who knew how much time she had wasted just lying here? When she spoke (*thought*) to the computer, her words had been transmitted to the beings outside. *Find help.* A command.

black white black white black white

She attempted to speak to the – what were they? – the creatures outside. Make them understand that the pod was highly dangerous, that there was only a short amount of time before the chamber split and everything –

ends?

Yes, if you like. Can you help me?

She let the thought hang there, no longer certain if she was talking to the ship of the people outside.

She slept.

The days and nights cycled on.

black white black

People?

She awoke.

It was a city. Dear God, it was a city.

(God?)

There were buildings and flying things that looked like planes but not quite planes that she recognised. Below her, were – yes - people. They were unmistakably people by now, they had managed to

black white black white

evolve that much. Outside the pod, she was slowly beginning to realise, time had passed on at a terrific rate. Hundreds, thousands, millions of years.

They still sang to her. She was their only constant.

The thing that had been there at their very beginning.

That which had asked for help.

We serve.

That which had promised them death.

End?

She looked at the details for the chamber. It looked like she had just hours before the split became unmanageable. Hours for her. If the people were still here, the fallout from the explosion would kill them all. Hell, the explosion itself would kill them.

(hell)

black white black white

Hours for her.

Perhaps a few hundred years for them.

Go, get out of here. Leave me. Get away.

But we serve. You have promised us death.

The people continued to sing, to bow, to worship.

(war ship)

They wouldn't leave. The days and nights and weeks and months and years cycled on, and they would not leave. They were trapped, bound to her as much as she was trapped in the pod itself.

The crack in the chamber had widened. Amelia glared at it, the image – of a padlock sliding into place – rising up again in her mind. There was still no way that she could escape the pod, not at the very least without widening the crack, without guaranteeing the explosion that would destroy all life on this planet, life that wasn't even here this morning.

It's been here for three million years; you're the intruder.

The timelines of that didn't quite add up, but Amelia took the point. The image of the padlock wouldn't go away. It was as if she –

She sighed. It was an entirely involuntary action, breath leaving her as she finally came to the realisation she'd been struggling towards for hours. Perhaps she hadn't been struggling at all; perhaps she had been avoiding this.

The door looked wrong because it was being locked from the inside. It wasn't to protect her from the days and nights; it was to protect the days and nights from her.

She asked the computer. Could the chamber be sealed?

Yes, but –

Will I have to be trapped in with it?

...

She had never heard an awkward silence from a computer before.

black white

Amelia told the computer to do what it needed to do. She could feel the air levels drop as it redirected power from one part of the pod to another.

Will this be enough? Will the pod contain the blast?

Yes. Just give the command. But only at the last minute.

The people lived their lives. The cities had expanded. Amelia was amongst them, forgotten.

5.

4.

Amelia remembered holding hands. A kiss, a final embrace before she got on the ship. A promise to see one another again.

3.

2.

She looked out at the people. The people bowed to her. She closed her eyes.

1.

Let there be light, she thought.

And there was.

PLENTY MORE PEBBLES

Margaret stepped back from the window, rather too quickly. She had been staring outward for nearly five minutes, her thoughts unfocussed, when a movement from the pavement below had caused her to look down. She swore softly, uncertain that she had been seen. Her foot knocked against the still open suitcase she had left on the floor. The last time she had stayed in this town had been over ten years ago, when her mother had helped her pack. Her clothes had been somewhat different then. There had been three dresses, all cotton, with a floral print and handmade by her grandmother and sent over from Ireland. There had also been a little straw hat, Margaret remembered now, which even then had seemed to her like a ludicrously expensive indulgence.

Margaret frowned, a crease forming an exclamation mark that rose from between her eyebrows. Today's suitcase contained mainly underwear. Yes, there was a dress – again, a cotton one, and again, a floral print. This one however had not been made for her by her grandmother, who had been dead now for nearly three years. Instead this dress had been bought for her by the man who had refused to hold her hand as they travelled down on the very busy train, hardly speaking to her at all until after they had left the station, and even then only to tell her to wait outside the hotel while he checked in. Now, he was back outside, walking the streets, looking for – in his words – a suitable place to eat. This time the ludicrous indulgence in her suitcase was a pair of stockings, which he hadn't given her. He didn't even know about them. She had bought them last week. She had thought, in some clumsy, unformed way, that they might be a nice surprise for him.

Cautiously, she stepped back to the window, noting without much surprise that the promenade was empty again. She wished that she had closed the curtains, and considered doing so now. But the damage had already been done. She looked out toward the sea again. Sunset had taken hold now, angry reds bleeding into the clouds. The promenade was still dark – the electric lighting hadn't been switched on yet – and the silhouette of the pier crouched black and low against the sea. It looked like the rain had followed them down from London. When Mr Lancaster (*William*, she reminded herself with a touch of wonder) had first suggested coming down to Brighton for the weekend, the idea had immediately taken hold of her with an almost inescapable sense of longing. Up until that point, she reflected, nothing had happened between them, not really. But that was rather the point: the 'nothing', it seemed to her, was a real, tangible thing, and it was always truly happening – *nothing has happened*. She watched the path of a raindrop as it trickled down the windowpane while she struggled to fix this concept in her head. For the past few months, the office that she had shared with Mr Lancaster (*William*) had been absolutely filled with – yes, with nothing, an absence, a moment before a something. It was there in the musk of the aftershave he wore, when he leaned into her whilst checking her shorthand, his chest pressed firmly against her back. And it was certainly there when his hand dropped onto her knee and simply rested there. Last week, when that same hand had begun to graze her thigh, the only hand apart from her own to reach that high, the whole room had been screaming with the weight of Nothing. Even now, sitting alone in this hotel room, Margaret wondered what might have happened if she had asked him to stop. Somehow, she doubted that the answer was: nothing. But to ask him to take his hand away had felt somehow – rude. Impolite. Was that a good enough reason to let his hand go wherever he wanted it to, to let him kiss her outside a pub that was not, no matter how much he claimed otherwise, on his way home?

The real reason she had allowed all these things to happen, the real reason she was now sitting on a strange bed, was a very simple one. Banal, even. Certainly not worthy of any defence, should she ever be asked to provide one. Simply put, she enjoyed the attention, she had enjoyed the kiss. She suspected (she *knew*) that she was far too young for him. Still just nineteen, while he was certainly in his forties (*in his fifties*, that maddeningly calm voice in her head corrected her), but she supposed that this was part of the attraction. If anyone had asked her if Mr Lancaster was actually attractive, she would have been genuinely confused by the inquiry: it wasn't for her to say. But even so, something about the mere fact of his attention excited her. She idly wondered how many women before her had felt the same way, and she pushed the traitorous thought down.

She looked around the room now, uncomfortably aware that she was doing nothing other than waiting. How often had this room been filled with Nothing, she asked herself (*before or after*, the voice demanded implacably). She noticed a dark patch on the wallpaper behind the bed, and it took her slightly too long to realise that it was the residue of many accumulated heads resting against the wall. Brylcreemed scalp after Brylcreemed scalp, each man seemingly choosing the same side of the bed, closest to the door (*all the better to make a quick exit*, the calm voice suggested).

There was a hesitant tap on the door. 'You can come right in,' Margaret called out. 'I'm on my own.' There was a pause before the door opened. The figure stood in the doorway, lighting glinting in her hair in much the same way as it had when Margaret had first seen her standing under the streetlamp just a few moments ago. Finally, Margaret realised that her visitor was waiting to be admitted entry. Sitting on the bed, she suddenly felt very exposed (*like a slattern*, she thought suddenly, before wondering exactly where *that* word had come from). As casually as she was able, Margaret stood, offering her hand in greeting. 'Hello, Mrs Lancaster. It's good to see you.' She was quite pleased with herself: her voice only shook once.

Ten minutes passed, in which they had smoked two cigarettes apiece, and spoken little. At some point, Mrs Lancaster had sat next to her on the bed, and Margaret had fought an instinct to spring a safe distance away from her. In a tone that sounded almost like she was merely making polite conversation, Mrs Lancaster asked how Margaret knew who she was. Margaret explained that William (*Mr Lancaster*, she amended, now that she was in his wife's presence) kept a photograph on his desk. 'Do you think I'm a fool, Miss Shaw?' Mrs Lancaster asked suddenly, and this sounded so much like an honest inquiry than an attack, that Margaret was temporarily lost for an answer. 'Nothing's happened,' Margaret said finally, weakly, and when Mrs Lancaster didn't reply, she continued, almost gabbling. 'I know that sounds like a lie. We've only kissed. This weekend was supposed to be …'

The older woman cut her off with a wave of her hand, and Margaret was immensely relieved. She hadn't quite had time to work out what the end of that sentence would have been. 'Oh, I don't doubt that,'

Mrs Lancaster told her. 'I believe you about that. I'm talking about something different. I'm asking a sincere question. Do you think I'm a fool? Letting William gallavant around?'

Margaret was about to answer, to say something to the effect that it probably wasn't Mrs Lancaster's choice or even within her control as to whether or not her husband cheated on her, before realising that she, Margaret, had at some point thought exactly that, and she decided not to answer.

Mrs Lancaster continued. 'William is a creature of habit. The same hotel. The same room. The same sort of girl.' (She gave Margaret an odd smile at this point, which seemed oddly affectionate). 'The same doctor when ...' She turned away, looking toward the window. 'Vivian – that's our daughter – has often said she wanted a little brother or sister to play with.' There was a very long pause, her jaw hardening. Margaret watched her, waiting for her to continue, noticing the way Mrs Lancaster's hair fell on her shoulders. Margaret wasn't aware you could describe the word *striking* to describe a person's beauty, but it was the word she was struggling for now. How, she wondered, could William (*Mr Lancaster*) ever risk losing this woman for a little girl like her? Sitting at the end of this bed, she had never felt more like a little girl.

Finally, Mrs Lancaster exhaled, and continued as if she hadn't stopped talking at all. 'William isn't skilled at meeting his responsibilities.' Another pause, another glance up, their eyes briefly meeting. 'But I suppose you already know that.' She stood, crushing her cigarette into a little steel ashtray that, for some reason, was screwed into the bedside table. *Not the only thing that gets screwed in here*, the voice chimed in, and Margaret had to clamp her mouth shut before it betrayed her with hysterical laughter. Mrs Lancaster walked to the window, as Margaret herself had done less than half an hour before. 'Such a lovely town,' she remarked. 'A shame to spend a weekend here and never see further than a bedroom.' Margaret allowed herself a slight nod. She still wasn't entirely sure what she should be doing, what her correct response should be. Mrs Lancaster didn't notice; she was still speaking. 'This is the first time I've followed him down here. I'm not sure why I did this time.' She frowned, momentarily lost in thought. 'He doesn't even bother to hide his affairs from me anymore. At least, he doesn't put in the effort. Invoices and bills to be found. He booked this room in the name of Mr and Mrs Lancaster.

Did you know that?' She glanced back at Margaret, who shook her head slowly. 'So it was an easy enough matter to come up here. I just told the receptionist that I'm his wife. Which I am, of course,' she added suddenly, with an odd sideways grin, as if that was a piece of information that Margaret had somehow forgotten. 'I still don't know what to do. Perhaps I'm afraid. Do you understand being afraid?' Margaret, who had hardly felt any other emotion since first seeing Mrs Lancaster, nodded mutely.

She knew she wasn't the first secretary that had come down with him for the weekend, not by a long shot. When she had been promoted to the position of his personal secretary after the previous one had to leave suddenly (to look after an aunt in Bath, apparently) she had already told herself that nothing was going to happen, partially because she didn't want to be yet another girl who fell under his charms, but mostly because she honestly thought there was nothing that he would want from her. But of course, as he had begun to pay more attention to her, she had found herself wanting to impress him, to catch his eye. Somehow, it had all begun to feel harmless. But it wasn't harmless, not at all, and the evidence was standing by the window.

Mrs Lancaster turned to Margaret, and smiled. A genuine, beautiful smile, and in that moment, Margaret wanted nothing else in the world than to stop hurting her. 'I didn't know what I was going to do tonight,' Mrs Lancaster said. 'I thought perhaps I would confront the pair of you together, although I have no idea what I thought that might achieve. I have my daughter to think of. I do have one friend who managed to ...' – the word came out with difficulty – 'divorce her husband. But I've hardly seen her since.' She walked back from the window, and sat down again. 'I even had a silly moment when I thought I might kill him. You too, of course. That didn't last long. I still don't know why I decided against it. Perhaps I don't want to hang for him. Perhaps I still love him.' She looked at Margaret again, a grim, cynical smile. 'I do, you know. I think perhaps I was afraid.'

The night was much darker now. All the red had gone from the sky, and the moon was behind a scud of clouds. The lights on the pier had all been switched on, and they twinkled prettily in the damp air. Mrs Lancaster gestured to a figure walking alone on the promenade, a dot of amber glowing at his mouth. Margaret stiffened slightly. 'Time for dinner,' Mrs Lancaster said. 'I wonder if he's booked for three.' Margaret was certain she could hear laughter in her voice.

FREE

Curley took a deep breath and told himself that he had delayed the inevitable for far too long. So thinking, he launched himself forward, and trotted down the dusty path.

Summer was at its height now, and there was a comfortable buzzing in the air, and in the distance, the not unpleasant scent of manure. That made him think of the farm, and sure enough, as he glanced over to his left, there it was – about six miles away, with a single plume of grey cotton smoke snaking lazily from the chimney. He wondered if he'd be able to recognise any of the animals in the yard, but it was impossible to see at this distance, even when he squinted.

After a short while, he came to the edge of the woods. Again, he had to steel himself: once he had transgressed this border, there would be no turning back: he was quite obviously an outsider. He swallowed hard. If he was not able to explain his presence satisfactorily, if the inhabitants of these woods decided that they did not wish to let him leave unharmed, he could very well end up dead in a ditch somewhere – just as his mother had always warned him.

Trying very hard not to think about it too much, Curley pushed himself forward, and walked into the woods. He was startled by just how immediately the warmth of the sun vanished. The leaves of the trees gave a significant amount of cover, and already he was shaking in the cold. His ears became even pinker than they were normally. The daylight had fled, almost as if it were scared.

Two wolves were standing in his way. He could tell from the tension in their haunches that they were getting ready to spring, and despite every instinct screaming within him to flee, he forced himself to stay as still as possible. If he panicked now, if he tried to run away, the wolves would doubtless fall on him in seconds and rip him to shreds. He put as much effort as he could into staying completely still, and waited for the wolves to tell him one way or the other what he should do next. He was still shivering, and he hoped that the wolves would not interpret that as fear. He was fairly certain that if he looked back over his shoulder right now he would see two additional wolves blocking his exit. Whatever happened now, choice was largely not a luxury that remained open to him.

The two wolves in front of him were not exactly the same as one another. The one to his left was slightly older with more grey hair, but was clearly the stronger of the two. It was this one that was regarding Curley carefully with pale yellow eyes. 'You're off the beaten track, aren't y', little one?' he asked, a slight chuckle to his voice.

Curley wanted to answer, but didn't trust his own voice: if he tried to speak, he would surely only manage a high-pitched squeal. So he simply nodded. The wolf nodded back, seemingly satisfied with that much. 'Our master is very keen to see you. It's been a long time.' The two wolves sidestepped slightly, opening up the pathway. Curley looked at them both in confusion, and the younger wolf drew his lips back in a snarl. The older wolf spoke in an overly polite tone: 'Please. Go ahead.' Curley looked at them both again, fully expecting that they would both suddenly and without warning spring on him and sink their teeth into his flesh.

But neither of them moved, except for a slight inclination of the head from the older wolf, reminding Curley that he should step forward. Heart thumping wildly in his chest, he did so. It seemed to take an eternity to move between them. He could hear them panting, and the smell of their sweat filled his nostrils. He wanted nothing more than to run away screaming, but knew that if he did so, no matter what their orders from their master were, their instincts would take over, and they would simply tear him into bloody strips before he had the chance to get even a few yards, gorging on his flesh.

'Come on,' the younger wolf said suddenly, making Curley jump. 'Chop, chop – we haven't got all day.' Curley nodded, and forced his little legs to move faster, still without panicking into a run. As they walked, Curley was dimly aware of even more wolves peering at them from behind the trees. He kept his mouth clamped tightly shut, certain that if at any point he opened his mouth – even just to take a breath – he would start moaning in distress.

Despite his all-consuming panic, it wasn't too long before they arrived at their destination: a large clearing, encircled by a disparate border of trees. The older wolf padded past Curley, and without bothering to look behind him, muttered a command that Curley should stay where he was.

Curley obeyed, and watched as the older wolf walked up to the darkest part of the clearing, a huge pile of twigs and leaves, a sole shaft of weak sunlight striking directly into the heart of it. There was yet another pair of wolves standing proudly on either side, with what looked like a clump of oily rags balanced precariously on the pile of twigs.

As Curley watched, the older wolf bowed his head to the bundle of rags and murmured something. There was a moment's pause, and the rags shifted. Curley could hear harsh, ragged breaths. The two wolves on either side sat slightly stiffer, slightly taller. It was only then that Curley understood what he was looking at: the pile of twigs and leaves was a throne. And the clump of rags was not a clump of rags at all, but an animal. In fact, he was looking at the undisputed leader around here. The Respected Elder. Known in local legend as The Big Bad Wolf.

The Big Bad Wolf took what felt like an agonisingly long time to get himself to a proper sitting position. It was quite unpleasant to watch. His skin was a furious red, and there were only a couple of patches of skin that were still covered in hair or fur. His breathing was shallow and hitched, stuttering in between every huff and puff. His right eye was a milky white ball, and it looked to Curley like it had sunken deep inside the Big Bad Wolf's skull.

Once the Big Bad Wolf had managed to sit, he regarded Curley impassively with his one good eye. The clearing was filled with the sound of his rasping breaths, which now suddenly and startlingly stopped. Curley stared, hardly daring to interrupt the sudden silence with his own breathing, crazily convinced that just by arriving here he had somehow shocked the Big Bad into his death throes. He was wildly wondering what on earth he could say to convince the remaining wolves to let him go – even if he had accidentally just killed their leader – when the silence was replaced by a hissing whisper. It took Curley far too long to realise that the Big Bad Wolf was actually talking to him. He strained forward to listen, but it was no good: he couldn't hear anything that was being said. Curley began to panic, but his concern – on this aspect, at least – was premature: one of the wolves on the side of the Big Bad had leaned in to listen, and they now repeated to Curley everything that was being said. Apparently, they were well used to visitors having problems hearing their leader clearly. Curley blinked a couple of times, rapidly. He wondered how many visitors the Big Bad had had. And how many had been allowed to leave.

'My lord is insulted by your presence,' the second wolf said, speaking for his master. Curley did not reply. It didn't feel like his voice would be welcome at this point. 'He says, how dare you even face him,' the second wolf added. Again, Curley did not respond. He wanted to be sure that once he did actually start talking, he would not be interrupted. He would only get one chance to speak, and he did not want to waste the opportunity.

'This is your fault. Do you deny it?' Now that he was closer to the Big Bad Wolf, he could see even more clearly (not that he wanted to) the damage the events of last summer had inflicted on the wolf's body. The furious blotching and burns were even more obvious now, and Curley could see a point, high on the wolf's ribcage, where the skin looked particularly porous, as if applying any pressure whatsoever would make the chest collapse and fall.

'You did this,' Big Bad snarled, using his own voice at last. 'You should have killed me when you had the chance.' Once again, Curley said nothing. He wanted to protest, to explain that none of this was his fault, that if the Big Bad Wolf had left Curley and his friends alone, then none of them would be in this situation now. But how could he explain any of that to the wolf, in a way that the wolf would understand? For two weeks at the end of last summer, Big Bad had terrorised Curley and his family. He could have eaten any animal that he wished, but for some unfathomable reason, he had set his sights (and his taste buds) on Curley and his brothers. All of the defence systems that Curley's brothers had attempted had failed, utterly. Certainly sticks and straws had been futile. And so it had been, with almost crushing inevitability, that Curley's two younger brothers had sought refuge at his house, because it had been Curley alone who had had the foresight to build a house made of bricks. Because his brothers had refused to look *ahead*, because they refused to take responsibility for their own lives, it was Curley's nice house, in the nice part of the village, which had had to contend with the arrival of an insane wolf on the doorstep.

Despite all the local rumours, Curley could not accept responsibility for what had happened next. After all, it was not his fault (as he was sorely tempted to mention now) that the wolf had chosen –

despite all protests and obstacles – to *still* attempt to gain entry to Curley's home. And through the chimney, too! No matter that Curley had lit the fire less than half an hour before, and that there was a cauldron of boiling hot water waiting for him at the end of his descent. Curley remembered all of this, and seriously considered reminding Big Bad of it too, but thought it wise to keep his mouth shut, to remain silent until asked flat out by the Big Bad himself exactly what he was doing here.

When the question finally did come, Curley took one moment to steel himself. If he faltered now, if he hesitated or even stuttered, he was surely done for. It was important that he kept on speaking, that he didn't allow the Big Bad Wolf to interrupt him in any way.

'You're the only one who can help me,' Curley said. 'If I had any options, believe me, I would have taken them. But I don't know what else to do. I'm desperate.'

The Big Bad Wolf's eyelids fluttered erratically for a moment, and Curley realised he was trying to blink, but was physically unable to. 'Say that again,' he said at last, in his thin, rasping voice. Curley said it again. There then followed a long, spooling silence during which even the birds of the forest apparently felt too awkward to speak out.

After far too long, Curley felt that perhaps he was being expected to embellish and expand on his story, and so he did, curiously losing his nervousness as he did so, becoming ever more confident as he fell deeper into his story.

'You know what happened. You were pursuing my brothers and I – yes, yes, I know it's in your nature, but equally it's in our nature to not want to be eaten. Yes, I'm fully aware of our supposed higher purpose, but even when that final end comes, it's often sudden and without warning. None of us want to die after being chased in terror all day, and we don't want to perish at the hands of tooth and claw.'

Curley swallowed hard, painfully aware that he was beginning to mix up his metaphors. He suspected however that it didn't actually matter all that much. 'We tried to take control of our lives, to lock ourselves away,' he continued. 'But you blew our houses ...' he broke off suddenly, squealing in fear: Big Bad had let out a harsh, impatient snarl. 'Oh, get on with it, little piggy,' the wolf snapped. 'As you rightly say, I was there.' The wolf settled down again, wincing in pain. Curley nodded slowly. 'As you say. Well, my brothers fled to my house. Which, luckily, was made of bricks.'

'Nothing lucky about it, bacon-arse. You're the smart one. A brick house. With a working chimney and flue. All constructed within a number of hours. And you, without opposable thumbs. You must've been feeling pretty pleased with yourself. Particularly when you tricked the Big Bad Wolf into your pot of burning hot water.' The wolf grinned nastily, and for the first time Curley saw that two of his teeth were missing. 'I ... don't... I don't feel pleased with myself,' Curley protested. 'It wasn't me that got you hurt. You were the one breaking and entering.'

'Your property, your laws, eh?' the wolf said softly, watching Curley balefully. Curley tensed, wondering if the Big Bad was going to get up and start snarling again. He was surely far too weak to leap up at the pig, but he still had his two commanders at his side, and neither of them had fallen into a vat of boiling water: they were both strong and lean and mean.

The Big Bad Wolf seemed lost in thought for a moment, then jerked his head to one side. The second commander leaned forward and scratched his master below the ear. The Big Bad sighed in satisfaction, then returned his attention to Curley. 'Tell me, then. What appears to be the problem? And why am I, of all creatures, your solution?' A new thought appeared to form in his one eye at this very moment, although Curley felt certain it was the thought that the Big Bad Wolf had been leaning toward all this time: 'And what makes you think I'm going to help you?'

Curley didn't say anything for a very long time, gathering his thoughts. Once he had said what he wanted to say, there would be no turning back.

'The thing is. My brothers came to me in their hour of need. In their moment of terror. As they fled from you. They escaped to the house of bricks, the house that I built. Because their own houses – of straw, of twigs – were not fit for purpose. They fled to my house, and we closed the door on you. And you huffed, and you puffed ...'

'And I burned.' Again, that nasty grin.

'Uh, yes. That was a year ago.'

Curley said nothing more. And after a moment, he didn't need to. Realisation, gleeful and delighted, brightened the wolf's face. 'And now ...

they won't leave! You're stuck with them. They abandoned their own houses, moved in with you… and now you can't rid of them.'

Curley nodded unhappily, and looked to the ground as the other wolves started to yelp in hysterical, delirious laughter.

'This, dear boy, 'is exactly why it's a mistake to help those who fail to help themselves.' Curley didn't answer. This morning, he had not been confident that he would survive until nightfall. If a sermon from the wolf was the worst that he would have to endure, then so be it.

'Right then,' the Big Bad said with renewed energy, 'What do you want me to do?'

The question took Curley somewhat by surprise. Not because he was unprepared for it – this was why he had come into the forest in the first place, and he knew exactly what it was he wanted the wolf to do – but because he hadn't entirely expected the wolf to offer his services quite so easily. He glanced cautiously at the other wolves, still expecting that at any moment they would attack. It was clear from their expressions that they fully expected to be ordered to do as much any time now.

'I want … I want you to scare them away?' Curley had wanted it to sound like a statement rather than a question, but was unable to keep the upward inflection out of his voice. Now that he had said it out loud, it sounded like a genuinely foolish idea. But he was afraid to lose any momentum, so he carried on speaking, as quickly as he could. 'They're always there. They never leave. You could… you could just turn up and scare them.'

Big Bad glanced at both of his generals, who gifted him with a non-committal look. Curley, although not a wolf, could decipher their response easily enough: *up to you*. There was not any version of this scenario where they feared for their master or for themselves. Big Bad, however, was more careful, and stared, unblinking, at Curley. 'How do I know it's not a trap?' he demanded. 'I've been burned before,' he added with a sly chuckle.

If Curley was supposed to respond to Big Bad's joke with laughter, he was too nervous to pick up on his cue, and in any case was already providing a sincere answer before the thought occurred to him. 'It's not a trap, honest. And look – there's just us, three little pigs. Whereas, you …' He gestured around, not feeling the need to finish his sentence. There were at least thirty wolves watching their conversation right now. He was certainly outnumbered.

Big Bad craned his neck to one side again, and once again, one of his generals scratched him. 'Alright,' he said slowly, an amused tone in his voice. 'If I do this, what's in it for me?'

Curley had a few more specifications to add to his request before they got to the subject of payment, and oddly enough now that they had got this far, he felt able to be a lot more bold: if they were going to kill him, then they were going to kill him, and a bit of bolshiness on his part wasn't going to make that more likely. He hoped.

'After today, you don't ever come near my home again,' he said, surprised at how firm and steady his voice suddenly was. He wondered how much longer that would continue.

The wolf nodded, to indicate that he understood. Curley continued. 'And after today, you don't go near my brothers' homes.'

As much as his lack of eyebrows would allow it, Big Bad's eyes narrowed. 'I thought they didn't have homes of their own?' he snarled.

'I'm working on that,' Curley answered. He hoped that his nervousness didn't betray him at this point: it was true that he had been looking for replacement abodes for both his brothers, and in any case if the wolf did in fact scare them out of his house, it was hopefully obvious that they'd have to live elsewhere.

The wolf fell back onto his throne, breathing heavily. The conversation had clearly exhausted him, and Curley was for the first time beginning to comprehend that it would not be the Big Bad Wolf himself that would be scaring his brothers from his house of bricks; it would be one of his generals. Curley wondered if they could be trusted in the heat of the moment.

The wolf had taken to whispering again, and one of the wolves at his side was repeating his words to Curley.

'So terrible to see a family fall apart like that,' the wolf said, sneeringly. 'You'd be happy to throw your brothers to the wolves just because they hog the bathroom in the morning? Because they always take the last biscuit? Such an evil idea. It's only a pity you didn't think of it first.'

'I ...' Curley began, and stopped.

'What do you mean, I didn't have the idea first?' Confusion meant that he had quite forgotten to be afraid. There was a flutter of movement at his side, but he didn't quite dare look that way. One of the wolves at the side of Big Bad began to laugh, quite deliriously.

'You see, you're not the only swine who wanted the place to yourself,' the first wolf said, this time apparently without any prompting from Big Bad.

Finally, Curley dared a look to his side, and saw, flanked by a gang of even more wolves, his two brothers.

'What ... the *hell* are you doing?' he hissed.

'Oh, you're a fine one to talk,' retorted Blake. 'You were going to sell us out to the wolves, were you?'

'I just wanted you out of my house! I was going to find you new places! What's *your* excuse?'

And to that, apparently, Blake and Tomas had no answer.

Curley began to squeal in indignation. 'I can't ... *believe* what I'm hearing here! Yes, my plan was risky, but I wasn't *actually* trying to get my own brothers killed!'

'What do you call this?'

'This? This was negotiating! You wouldn't get out of my home!'

'You should've asked!'

'I did – several times!'

'And this is how you treat family, is it?'

'Oh, you're a fine one to talk!'

'Excuse me.'

The three little pigs stopped. The last voice to speak hadn't belonged to any of them. It had been soft and quiet, but it had very easily commanded their attention. The Big Bad Wolf was grinning, saliva drooling generously from his jaws. 'I hate to break up the family reunion – after all, it's not often I get dinner *and* a show – but I think it's time for this little feud to end.'

Tomas – always the cheeky one – risked an attempt at a joke. 'Does that mean we get to be friends, and no-one gets eaten?'

The wolves looked at him, uniformly, with contempt. Tomas looked down at the ground, and didn't say anything else.

The Big Bad Wolf pulled himself to his full height one last time. 'So, how about it, boys?'

Curley blinked several times, not entirely sure if he had missed something. 'How – how about what?'

The wolf was beginning to climb down from his throne. 'For old time's sake,' he explained, 'I'm going to give you a head start. All three of you. I give you my word that none of us will run after you for – ooh, at least half an hour. That sound fair?'

The laughing from all the wolves echoed around the treetops, suggesting that it probably wasn't even close to fair. 'You better get started,' the Big Bad suggested. 'I do love the thrill of the chase.' He looked at each of the pigs in turn. 'Who's brave enough?'

Some of the wolves stepped to one side, and the three little pigs blinked at each other in confusion, nobody quite knowing what to do.

Nothing happened.

The Big Bad Wolf licked his lips. 'That's twenty nine minutes,' he said.

The pigs ran.

*

'Not that way!'

Curley's brothers stopped; or at least Blake stopped very suddenly, and Tomas collided into the back of him. They had been running for nearly an hour now. They hadn't seen a wolf in nearly ten minutes, although they could always hear their howling. It sounded very much like they were surrounded.

Blake got to his feet and stared at Curley. 'What do you mean? Home is that way! We need to get home!'

Curley considered arguing the point about whose home it was, but decided that now wasn't the time. 'You're an idiot if you think the Big Bad Wolf hasn't got one of his soldiers standing at the door waiting for us. We're not going to be able to go home anytime soon,' he warned.

The sound of wolf laughter was getting closer.

'Well, we're going to have to find shelter soon,' Tomas said frantically.

Curley pointed in the opposite direction to where his brothers had been heading. 'There's another house we can hide in. For the moment.'

Blake scoffed. 'A house? Here in the forest?'

Curley had already started trotting away, hoping that his brothers would follow him. He had been heading this way all the time, and was very happy he hadn't got confused: it was well known just how easy it was to get lost in these woods. 'Yes. It's a bit of a risk, but we don't have much of a choice. Look, here it is.'

The three little pigs stopped in their tracks despite the far-too-close sound of the approaching wolves.

'That's a house?' Tomas squeaked.

'It's not made of bricks,' Blake suggested.

'It's not even made of straw,' agreed Tomas. 'Or twigs,' he added, not wishing to share the rule of three with anyone.

'No,' muttered Curley, as the occupant of the house came out to greet them.

'Hello,' he said. 'I'm sorry to bring the wolves to your door, but we need to hide for the night. Can you help?'

The little old lady smiled. 'Of course I can, my lovely ones. I've put the oven on special. Come in, come in.' She waited for them to walk over the threshold before closing the door on the sound of the angry wolves. 'Now, tell me,' she asked. 'Would any of you boys like any gingerbread?'

THE MAN WITH CLEAR GREY EYES

The Reverend John Peters shook hands with the last of his congregation, and let out a deep breath. He didn't know why he still got so tense; he'd been with this parish for over eight years now, and he knew in his heart and soul that they accepted and trusted him. Now in his fifties, he no longer had the problem of being judged 'too young' to lead a flock in their faith, and no longer had to deal with the fascinated glances when a newcomer discovered that he was one of only a few hundred married Catholic priests in the world. That, at least, was not a conversation he had to have with his parishioners any more.

Instead, he guided them in marriages, funerals and christenings, as well as several services a week. He knew that there were several priests – even ones in cities – who had cut down the amount of services to just a few a week, but for his church, he wished always to be available. Such dedication came at a cost, however, and he always appreciated the moments of peace God gifted him with. He glanced around the street, satisfied that his day was, for the most part, done.

As a priest, there was no such thing as a quiet time of year – just times that were slightly less busy than extraordinarily busy times – but the fortnight before autumn harvest was about as close as he could hope for. He breathed in the night air, turned on his heel to go back into the church, and locked the door behind him.

He had started to walk down to the altar when he spotted the man at the front of the church. He wasn't sitting at a pew, nor was he waiting shiftily by the confessional. Instead, he was peering at the inscription underneath the Second Station Of The Cross, and when he heard John approach, he turned and gave a genial little wave. John waved back, judging that he had just enough time for whatever this chap wanted to talk about before he would need to eat. He did not sense that he had any need to worry.

John had developed three very valuable techniques during his time with the church, and he was able to employ the last two of them now. The first tool of his trade was of no use to him at this moment, because he was walking towards the man, not away from him, and this was the wrong direction: John had learned very early on that his day to day existence would be a lot less exhausting if he made sure to always be in motion, always be walking, because the unfortunate truth was that if any of his parishioners ever saw him seated – having a coffee in the local tea-rooms, for instance – then they would take that as a welcome mat to talk at him for hours (and it often was hours) at a time. That in itself, he didn't resent or even mind: listening to those who needed to speak to him was hardwired into his job: it was, if you wanted to find a phrase for it, what he had been put on this earth to do.

But it was undeniable (*speak the truth and shame the devil*) that even some Christians could be selfish, and there were at least a few people in his parish who would, given the chance, far too easily monopolise his time - time that would be better given for instance to the boy who had been rejected by his own family even as he was suffering withdrawal symptoms, time that was sorely needed by the young Syrian couple who were desperately trying to find their way through the labyrinth of forms and identity papers, time that was valuable to the young girl who wanted to go to art school, but was never going to be able to afford it. None of these people were particularly good church-goers (they didn't even pretend to be), but Father John Peters and the church was there for them, no matter what their problem was. Not so much the Citizens Advice Bureau, but the Christian's Advice Bureau, as his verger, Mr Briars, liked to call it. John thought the pun awful, but it was apt, nonetheless.

So the trick as a busy priest was to keep moving. If whoever wanted to talk to you just wanted to talk to you because they simply wanted someone to talk to, they would soon give up, and find someone else: they didn't actually need a man of God. And John was pretty adept (at least he thought so) at detecting the people who were genuinely lonely or depressed, and these people he would stop and speak with. Everybody else: he'd just keep moving. Mostly, those who were not in absolutely dire straits would take the hint and leave him alone.

The man in front of him by the first pew did not appear to be in any desperate need – a little shabby and tired looking, perhaps, but there was nothing about him that set off John's radar for concern. On the other hand, John didn't think he'd ever seen this man in any congregation, so it was possible that he wouldn't be able to pick up on any signals anyway. It was also possible, of course, that this stranger was about to hold him up at gunpoint and rob the candlesticks (John had become a priest long after anyone seriously thought that the dog collar protected one from being a victim of crime). As he got closer, John had a surreptitious look around the church to see if the man had some kind of accomplice hiding in the shadows. But as far as he could tell, it was just the two of them. Well, the two of them and God, of course.

So the man in front of him now pretty much had him trapped: they were definitely going to have to have some kind of conversation. Which was where John's two other techniques were going to come in useful: for a start, he always (even when in constant, hurried motion) allowed himself at least forty minutes after each church service before he had fixed any other appointment or plan. Forty minutes, in other words, to allow for the unplanned or unexpected. John found that it made for a far less frustrating day if he had already made the assumption that he would never be allowed to get back to his own kitchen without some kind of delay (and so whenever his journey was uninterrupted it felt like a delightful gift), and such an assumption meant that he was never annoyed on the occasions he *was* delayed, and never felt the need to be continually checking his watch.

Which was what his third trick was all about – over the years, he had developed an almost flawless internal clock, and never wore a watch. Instinctively, he always knew what the time was, which had proven to be a very useful skill. On the occasion that he felt the need to test himself – surely he couldn't *always* be right? - he would guess at the time – and find, upon checking with somebody else's watch or his phone – that he was correct, to within a few minutes. So, all things considered, the Reverend John Peters was completely relaxed when the genial looking man in a shabby coat doffed his hat: the old guy looked happy enough, and there was still light in the sky. This wasn't going to take long at all.

*

The man drank deeply from his cup, and then looked at him. John had the impression that he – the man sitting opposite him – was appraising him, weighing him up, considering if John was a worthy – or even suitable – person to speak to. He had invited the man (who he now knew was called Dan) to his kitchen in the vicarage, where he busied himself making tea. The man had sat quietly, looking around with the same fascination that all his non-regular visitors did; the air of bemused – even mildly scandalised – surprise that he would have such real life, non-Christian, non-priesty things in his home as a TV guide, a selection of chocolate bars, or a boxset of the latest Scandi drama. Nobody ever said as much, but it was clear that they expected him to be sleeping on the floor, wrapped in thin sackcloth with no material goods to enjoy. He couldn't quite understand their thought processes, but he supposed that for his visitors, it was a similar experience to the times when he as a child had encountered one of his teachers in a shop in town, and been slightly overwhelmed by the idea that they existed outside of school.

He sat down, and offered one of the cups of tea to Dan. 'You said that you had a big favour to ask me?' he asked. Dan nodded rapidly, as if he had completely forgotten that he had said such a thing, and that he was grateful for John's reminder. He then, somewhat unexpectedly, produced an empty jam jar from his coat pocket and placed it with great care on the table. Just as gently, he then picked up the tea cup. John was reminded incongruously enough of the moment when Indiana Jones swapped a golden idol for a bag of sand. Dan swigged a mouthful of tea, winced – 'Hot,' he explained in an apologetic tone – and tapped the empty jam jar. 'I'd like you to take this for me,' he said. John leant forward, trying not to squint. As far as he could see, the jar was definitely empty.

John looked at Dan with a completely neutral expression on his face. He knew it was completely neutral; he had spent a fair amount of time practicing it in front of the mirror. In his line of work, one anticipated having many conversations that might worry, dismay or even disgust: if a part of a priest's job is to be a counsellor or confidante (and he believed that it was), then John considered it vital that he was capable of keeping his initial true reactions hidden – if people were concerned that they would be judged, then they might not talk to him at all. In a light, flat tone, he asked the obvious question. 'What would it be that I would be looking after?' he asked. Dan smiled.

'Do you believe in evil?' Dan asked mildly, and John relaxed, now knowing exactly how this was going to play out: Dan was in some way unwell, and needed guidance. Fortunately, he did not appear to be manic, although John was very aware that that could change at any moment. There was always a good number of individuals in every congregation who saw the world in very Old Testament terms, seeing Satan and all his followers behind every post-box. The Lost, Peters had taken to calling them, although his old mentor would simply refer to them as 'nutters'.

Usually, such people were harmless. Indeed, most of the time, there was very little to distinguish between the nervous looking man who clearly hadn't eaten properly in about a month and would follow John around the church as he collected the hymn books after the Tuesday morning service and raving about goblins, and the serious, humourless women who were at pains to let him know just how much they had sacrificed for their lord. It was always *their* lord, John had noticed. Not *the*, or even *our*, but *my*. A curious sense of ownership on a deity, he had always thought.

'Do *you* believe in evil?' he asked Dan at last. It was by far the wisest cause of action: John certainly had opinions – entire sermons in fact – on the subject of evil, but it was best that he learned (and pretty swiftly, too) exactly what *Dan* meant – or thought he meant – by the term. It was becoming pretty obvious that Dan was the first type of Lost: the person who worried about goblins, and was plagued by paranoia. John allowed himself a quick, causal glance around the kitchen, wondering where he had last seen his phone.

Dan held up the jam jar, where it caught the light. It wasn't particularly beautiful, but both men were distracted by it for a moment. 'This jar,' Dan said, holding the jar up in front of his face so that his eyes looked to John warped and misshapen, 'contains my soul. Do you believe me?'

John laced his fingers together in an attempt to underline that he was listening, and indicate that he understood that whatever Dan said was important. It was an awful, condescending gesture he had picked up in his university years studying psychology, but didn't appear to be able to rid himself of, and leaned toward Dan even more deeply. 'The real question,' he said, 'is do *you* believe it?'

In answer, Dan threw his arm out in an action usually to be seen on a bowler during a cricket match. John was already on his feet before he realised he was reacting. 'No!' he blurted out, but when he looked, the jam jar was still firmly in Dan's grasp. 'So you do believe,' Dan said lightly. 'At least a little bit.'

John sat back down. 'I was concerned about you smashing a glass jar in my home,' he protested.

Dan smiled. 'I believe you, thousands wouldn't,' he replied in an almost sing-song voice. He placed the jar back down on the table.

'I am a custodian of souls,' Dan said. He let that sentence hang in the air for a moment while John attempted to make sense of it, an attempt that was doomed to failure. Dan smiled kindly, and began to explain. 'When I asked you if you believed in evil, I suppose what I was really asking was if you believed in the devil, but I'm guessing I don't have to bother with that question.'

If it was true that Dan didn't have to ask the question, it was certainly true that John didn't need to supply the answer: while his belief in God was absolute and unwavering, he – like many of his colleagues in the priesthood – did not accept the old-fashioned concept of the existence of an actual, specific Satan – certainly not if what you meant by that was a cloven-footed devil with horns, or a expensively suited tempter with the looks and demeanour of Peter Cook. But it was clear that Dan *did* believe in the devil, and that if John just let him continue talking, he would explain further.

'The devil exists, and he lives amongst us,' Dan said with apparently very little interest in whether or not John thought him mad. 'I don't pretend to know all that you've covered in your studies to become a priest – I haven't really had the time to do the same lectures you will have done – but I can tell you that the devil trades immortal life in heaven for a human soul.'

Despite himself, John found the pull of a theological argument too strong (*resist temptation*, he told himself). 'Look, I'm afraid it doesn't work like that,' he began, but Dan silenced him with an impatient wave of his hand. 'It works exactly like that,' he retorted. 'I have traded the nebulous chance of eternal salvation for the concrete certainty of happiness down here on earth.'

Chancing another look for his phone, John decided that it would be futile to attempt to convince Dan to abandon his belief. 'Are you saying that you've met the devil? And you've sold your soul to the devil?' Dan gave two carefully separate nods, one for each question. 'If that's true, why do you still have your soul in a jam jar? And why are you – what did you call yourself – a custodian of souls?'

Dan fished in his pocket, and brought out a battered mobile phone. He studiously fiddled with some buttons – clearly not used to having to deal with such modern technology. Finally, he turned the screen to face John. It was a photograph, and John gazed at it in blank incomprehension for a moment, not entirely certain what he was looking at. The actual *details* of what he was looking at was clear enough – it was a collection of glass jars, at least half of which still had their original labels on them. The picture was slightly blurred (no prizewinning photographer was our boy Daniel), but it was obvious that all the jars in the picture were empty.

'So,' John began uncertainly, 'are these all other souls? Souls that you look after?' Dan nodded. 'I know you don't believe me,' he said, 'but that's exactly what they are. A soul has to be retained here on earth until the person dies. It can't be contained within the person themselves, but neither can it be taken from Earth. It has to be held... captive, if you like. Until the person in question dies. When that happens, a custodian – me - has to smash the glass, and so release the soul. Then – and only then – does it get collected by the devil.'

John stared at Dan for a moment, which may have looked to the latter as if he was trying to understand what had just been said, but in truth, John was just attempting to see if Dan's delusion in any way was a danger to anyone, and as far as he could work out, it wasn't. 'So it's your job to look after the souls between purchase and delivery,' he said carefully. He was itching to get up and find his own phone, but felt that even standing might upset Dan out of his currently calm demeanour.

'Somebody has to do it,' Dan replied, as if it was obvious.

'So,' John asked slowly, fully aware that to engage this man in conversation might encourage him more than was wise, 'how many souls do you ... look after?' Dan watched him carefully. Now it was he suspecting that he was being tested. Which, John supposed, he was.

'Nine hundred and eighty.' His eyes flickered slightly, and he went on: 'Actually, it's nine hundred and seventy six. But in conversations like this, I find it's always helpful to round up, don't you?'

All of this had not really answered John's main sticking point, the flaw in Dan's logic. The man was telling him that he had become the guardian of the world's souls, that people had sold their soul for fame and fortune, for love and luck, and now he, Dan, kept their souls in what was little better than jam jars in his garden shed. The man was clearly disturbed (was that the correct phrase? He was sure Nita at the mental health group had to keep on correcting him), but John, as ever, was unable to resist the pull of an argument. It was unlikely that this man would be able to respond to the simple clarity of common sense, but John felt the need to give it a go anyway. 'Don't you think ... I mean, isn't that number a trifle low? I mean, it's not even a thousand.'

Dan looked at him with what, incredibly, appeared to be ill-disguised contempt. 'Actually, I'd say the number was rather high. We're talking about people selling their immortal souls – damning themselves for eternity – for the chance of fifty years with some more cash in their pockets and a bit more sex? How stupid do you think people are?'

John, who had spent more than a few sermons speaking about the powerful allure of temptation, was somewhat taken aback.

'Why – how are you in possession of your own soul?' John asked, partially in an effort to change the subject at least partially, and also to try and find the gap in Dan's argument.

'I'm not going to trust it to another Custodian, am I?' Dan retorted. 'They might smash the glass too early.' John opened his mouth to ask exactly what *that* meant, but Dan continued. 'Yes, there are Custodians all over the world. It's what we do. We collect souls, we look after them until the time comes. When a soul is to be released, we smash the glass.' Dan drained his teacup. 'Mistakes happen; people's jars get broken too soon. I thought I'd be better off looking after my own.' Dan and John stared at the jam jar sitting on his kitchen table in silence, the situation feeling to John increasingly surreal.

'So,' John responded, not entirely certain why he was allowing this conversation to continue, 'what were you promised? What did you have to exchange your soul for?' The man gave him another of those looks – *do you really need to ask* – and smiled softly.

'What else?' he said at last. 'Her name was Imogen. I hadn't even heard of that name before I met her. Can you believe that?' John, who felt that on balance, that would be the least fantastical thing he would be asked to believe today, simply nodded. 'I was in love,' Dan continued slowly, appearing to put emphasis on each separate word.

'And did it work?' John found that if he had been asked to guess the man's answer at this point, he would have had no idea what was going to be said. The man looked into his empty cup for a long while. Finally, he nodded. 'Yes. She loved me. She was a good and faithful wife. She gave me beautiful children.' All of this was said in a flat, carefully emotionless voice. The man looked up to meet John's gaze, and momentarily blinked, almost as if it were he, John, that had the pale, penetrating stare. 'I won her heart, but it was a weak victory. I knew it was a lie. Even if she herself did not.'

John's internal watch reminded him that their forty minutes were up, although he suspected that their conversation was far from over. 'You said you needed a favour from me. What was that favour, Dan?'

For the first time, Dan looked upset, and then the expression vanished from his face as he willed himself into action. He placed a palm gently on top of the jam jar and slid it carefully across the table towards John. 'I want you to smash this,' he said. 'I want you to smash this and deliver my soul to the devil.'

*

It was a little after midnight. John closed the door behind him, not realising until now that he had been holding his breath until he let it out in deep exhalation. He had been very tense, the muscles in his body coiled (the phrase *fight or flight*, which he had not heard since school, rattled around in his brain). Now that he was in the shed behind Dan's house, he realised, he had been fully expecting a place stacked full of yellowing newspapers, a sink of decaying, stagnant dishwater. Either that, or something at the polar opposite: viciously scrubbed surfaces, everything wrapped in plastic. This house, however, seemed... normal.

It had taken John about two hours and three trains to cross town and find Dan's house, which had given him enough time to wonder why Dan had chosen him rather than any other priest who no doubt lived closer (*none of us shall question the call when it comes*, he thought to himself in an unformed, uncertain way).

John also had had enough time to brood over what Dan had said to him before he'd left him at the vicarage (there was, as always, the very real risk that all of this was an overly elaborate scam to get John out of the way so he could be robbed blind, but on balance he'd rather that happened when he wasn't around, and thank God that he didn't get hurt). 'I can't look after the souls anymore,' Dan explained. When John asked Dan what he meant, the older man said 'They're after me,' and then surprised them both by breaking up into helpless laughter.

'I'm sorry, I know how paranoid that sounds,' he said finally. '"They're after me!"', he repeated in a we're-all-mad-here voice while waving his hands. He grinned, and then let the grin disappear. 'But they *are* after me, Reverend. They're going to find me, and they're going to collect. I haven't kept my part of the bargain.'

In Dan's shed, John switched on the light feature on his phone (he had managed to find his phone before he left the vicarage), and swept it around the darkness. The jars — hundreds of them — twinkled in the gloom. Still, his mind wandered back to what Dan had told him.

'I have to keep up to date with the death notices, the what do you call it — the obituaries. Which isn't as easy to do these days, don't know if you know. Of course you know; look who I'm talking to. Well. When someone under my custody dies, it's my task to smash their jar. Release their soul to the devil.' Here, Dan leaned forward, and gripped both of John's shoulders in what could only be described as proud delight. 'Only: I haven't. I've kept the souls intact. If they have to stay in the jam jars until Judgement Day, then so be it. But the devil ain't having them.' His smile became wider. 'Fuck the devil!' His brow creased. 'Sorry, Reverend.'

John shrugged, watching Dan with burgeoning wonder. 'I suppose I applaud the sentiment, even if I can't officially condone the language.'

Dan released John's shoulders, his face still covered in beaming pride, and in that moment, John discovered with only mild surprise that he believed every word. 'But ... if you haven't released the souls you were supposed to, then — then you'll be in danger. And then it'll be someone else who smashes all the jars. It will all have been for nothing.' Dan gave him a look — *what do you think I've been trying to tell you?* — 'They'll find someone else. They always find someone else. It has to be a someone, a — what do you call it — ha! A human! The devil and his demons can only promise. They can't touch. But if they find me at home, they might... persuade me to smash the jars. I'm so weak these days. I might not resist. And I thought, if I bring this jar to you, and you smash it... then — well, I'll die, and be far away from the jars in my custody. Perhaps they won't find the souls for a little while.' John nodded slowly. It had already occurred to him that there was a fairly fundamental flaw in Dan's plan – if he was dead, then surely his house would be emptied and sold on, and a pile of old jam jars would be the first to get thrown away and chucked in the recycling. *Can you recycle souls?* he thought, before remembering there were several faiths that argued exactly that.

'You realise that if everything you're saying is true, then as soon as I break this jar, you're condemned to an eternity of damnation?'

It was Dan's turn to shrug. 'That's what I signed up to,' he said softly. John considered this quietly for a moment. 'Can I see the jars for myself? He asked at last.

'I can't go back,' Dan protested, a tinge of panic in his voice. 'If they – whoever they are – find me when I'm with the jars, then they might take everything. All at once.'

'No, I'm not asking that,' John said. 'Give me your address, and I'll go. Check things out for myself. You wait here.'

'And you'll smash the jar, right? As soon as you see I'm not lying, you'll smash the jar?'

'What will happen when I do? To your physical form?'

Dan shook his head in a *that's not what's important* kind of way. 'I'll die, that's all. I don't have to be here: you don't want to come back home to find a dead body on your living room floor.'

John opened the door to his lounge. 'Nonsense. If you're going to die anywhere, it may as well be on the couch. Go on. You've earned the rest.'

*

Now, standing in Dan's shed, John took the empty jam jar out of his coat pocket, and held it aloft, weighing it. It was entirely normal. Of course, it felt both heavy (as if it contained an invisible soul) or lighter than air (as if it contained an invisible soul). He raised the jar above his head.

He waited.

He lowered his hand slightly, noticing with a dull lack of surprise that he was no longer alone.

'Hello.'

John found that he was unable to speak in response. He decided to just nod, thinking that doing so might be enough for now. Apparently it was.

'Do you know who I am?'

The transformation in John, had there been anyone there to see it, was quite remarkable. Less than thirty seconds ago, he had been a middle aged man gripping a jam jar. Now he looked very old, and tears were flowing copiously down his cheeks. He nodded. He had never seen this woman before (because, after all, she did not truly exist), but he knew very well who she was.

She was next to him. A hand on his, gently making him lower the jar even further. It hung limply by his waist. 'I don't think you should do whatever it was you were thinking of,' she said softly. John nodded almost involuntarily. He didn't know what was more astonishing, the fact that this woman was here at all, or that she was able to touch him. In this moment, he had completely forgotten if she could still be correctly called a spirit if she had a corporeal form. Come to that, he didn't know if she could be called a spirit if she looked like someone who had never really lived. It appeared that her ability to make contact with him only went so far: she wouldn't be able to knock the jar out of his hand. He looked back up at her face, marvelling at her.

'I would have been thirty,' the woman said, answering the question that was forming on his lips.

John nodded. That seemed about right. He and Sadie had tried for about three years, soon after settling in at his first parish. The bright young vicar and his beautiful wife, it was surely God's will that a child – many children – would follow. They had avoided calling it a miracle when Sadie finally got pregnant, which was probably just as well, since that would surely have meant that he would have been required to call the car crash just two weeks later an act of God, and while his faith had been severely shaken – of course it had been – he wasn't prepared to do that.

The church had looked after him, loved him. It allowed him to grieve, and it allowed him to move to another parish, where there were no memories. But memories are ghosts, and occasionally, ghosts followed you.

The woman who was not his daughter sat on a chair he hadn't previously seen, and placed her hands carefully on her lap. She became serious, business-like. It was remarkable how much she looked like her mother. 'That,' she said, pointing directly at the jar in John's hands, 'is our property. If anyone smashes it, it will be one of us.'

'What difference does it make?' John asked. 'Surely the result is the same.'

The woman smiled thinly. 'There are ways. And means. Traditions. I know that a man of your station understands such things.' She looked around at the other jars. 'There are more souls to be collected, as well. Your friend hasn't labelled them properly. More work for the next person.'

John's palm felt sweaty on the glass of the jar. He was suddenly convinced he was going to drop it, no matter what. 'The next person?'

The woman clicked her tongue in impatience. Her image was still the same, but whatever she was, she was no longer pretending to be his daughter. 'We still need a Custodian,' she explained, as if to an idiot. 'There will still be people in this world whose greed and stupidity we can exploit. After that jar is smashed, we need someone else to look after this lot.' She smiled, unpleasantly. 'It won't take us long. It pays quite well.'

John placed the jar on the floor. 'Choose me.'

The woman who wasn't his daughter inclined her head slightly, in a pantomime to indicate that she hadn't heard properly. 'What do you mean?'

John got down on his haunches and tapped the lid of the jar. 'Choose me as the next Custodian. I'll take full responsibility for these souls. This jar – this jar is empty.'

'What?'

'It's a jar of mine from home. I left Dan's jar with him. He's keeping it safe.'

'You can't trick us, you can't deceive..'

'No trick, no deception. Just a deal.'

'A deal?'

John unscrewed the lid of the empty jar. 'Dan's soul. For mine.'

'If you're going to bargain your soul away, shouldn't be for something more precious than the salvation of a man you've never met?'

'I can't think of anything more precious.'

The woman studied him. John was fairly certain now that whatever this thing was, it was very far from human. But still, the expressions on her face were very human. She was considering her options.

'If we accept your deal, you'll take on his role? You'll do the job he failed at?'

John didn't answer. *No promises.*

He slid the jar towards her, feeling oddly like someone making a desperate move toward the end of a chess match. 'Come on. The soul of a man of God? That's got to be worth something.'

The woman who wasn't his daughter glanced at the collection of empty glass jars. 'You'll do what he did. You'll keep the souls here.'

John felt something is his chest loosen. 'Perhaps I will. But look. The possibility of being cheated out of these souls. Versus the *guarantee* of my soul. Anything could happen.' He tapped the jar, twice. 'I'm reliably informed I could get knocked down by a bus tomorrow.'

She allowed herself a smile.

*

It was coming up to three when he got back home. Under the circumstances, he felt that he deserved a taxi. He checked in on Dan, who was sleeping on the couch. Carefully, he placed his jar, now firmly sealed, next to Dan's jar in the cupboard under the sink. He would think of a safer place tomorrow; it wouldn't do for either of them to get broken.

After all, it had always been his God-given job to look after souls.

WHERE WOLF

Tonight was warm, with very little breeze, and for that Helena was grateful. It had been raining almost constantly over the last few weeks, and with that rain there had been bitter, cold winds. Fortunately, those winds seemed to have stopped now. She could smell honey on the mild breeze. It felt like the elements themselves were making an effort for her special day.

She looked around, still somewhat taken aback. She couldn't help feeling absurdly flattered; almost the entire populace of the village was here. Of course, there was no need for her to be flattered, not really – it was an expectation that everyone in the village who was able, who was at of age, and was not required to look after the children or the infirm, should be here. But even allowing for all of that, it felt like everyone here *wanted* to be here – that this wasn't a chore, or done simply to serve the tradition of the village.

She had rarely been up this high on the hill before – up until today, there had been no need for her to do so – and looked around her with interest. They were surrounded by an almost perfect ring of tall trees. She couldn't tell (and she had never asked) if that was a natural occurrence, or if they had been planted that way deliberately so as to hide the view from the townspeople below. Later events would indicate to her that the latter might be closer to the truth.

Everyone was dressed in the traditional gowns. She'd seen her own father wear the same gown at each coming of age ceremony for as long as she could remember. The population of the village was not all that big – less than two thousand at the last census – but that was still enough people to ensure that there were several coming of age ceremonies every year; sometimes, there could be as many as six in a single week. It was the same for every villager, their coming of age being celebrated by all those who had already passed through the ceremony before them, although it was different for men and women – boys had the ceremony at the age of fourteen, while the girls had to wait until they were eighteen, an injustice that Helena had long ago decided that she would attempt to rebalance when she herself was old enough. The inequality inevitably meant that there were some villagers – the males – who were officially adults despite still looking and behaving like children, whilst alongside them there were girls who would not be referred to as women despite essentially being such for nearly half a decade. But such was the oddity of life and nature, as her father would say: a mystery that the village could never hope to solve.

She was the only child in her family, and so this was the first direct experience she had had of the ceremony itself. But this was her ceremony, and therefore she was the youngest person here. The reason they were all here, to celebrate her coming of age. And now, standing amongst them, she felt for the first time the weight of that phrase: *coming of age.* Her age was coming, hurtling towards her at a terrifying speed.

Her father was speaking now, delighting the town with a string of amusing and suitably embarrassing stories about her childhood. He was a natural orator, seemingly a strong candidate for mayor, but the post had never interested him, and he had always felt that he would not be able to carry out the office successfully enough. The village had never really agreed with the assessment he had made of himself. They respected him, wanted to hear what he had to say on any given subject. Helena had always been vaguely aware – ever since she had been old enough to be aware of anything, really – that the respect that the town held for her father extended easily and comfortably to her. Just the mere fact that she was his daughter was enough to shield her, to protect her in the warm blanket of the town's affection and – yes, this much was true – their love. And it was their love that she felt now, thrumming off everyone she could see, a sense of almost unbridled expectation, waiting for the moment when she, Helena, would finally become one of them.

The night was full now, and soon the moon would appear above them. On other nights during the month, it would hang above them even when the sky was blue, long before night had truly descended, and the villagers would often incline a salute to it in thanks. The village always took the time to thank the moon; the moon was their mother, their protector, their giver of life. Tonight, the full moon would finally accept Helena as a sister.

Her father had ended his speech, and introduced Joseph, who tonight would lead them in their prayer. As he entered the clearing, the gathering inclined their gaze toward him as one. A tall man, he had allowed his hair to grow long, falling far past his shoulders, where it hung in black waves. For the past few years, during which he himself had come of age, he had distracted the eye of many a girl in the village. It had taken him some time to choose a companion, and a not insignificant reason was because it was clear to anyone (including – grudgingly – himself, if he was drunk and cheerful enough to admit it) that he was by far the most attractive man around. But there had only ever been one woman for him.

The ceremony proper was about to begin. Joseph nodded, almost breathless with excitement. Everyone started to prepare, shrugging off their gowns. Helena did the same, trying to not look too intently at Joseph's nakedness. After all, it wasn't as if she had never seen him before. They had become lovers almost a year ago. While they had never announced their relationship and were very discreet, Helena had quickly come to the conclusion that their relationship was something of an open secret in the village. After all, her own father was not a man from whom secrets could easily be kept.

As the villagers all threw off their gowns – some neatly folding them on the ground, some just throwing them aside – Joseph was still talking excitedly, sounding to Helena for once like the boy she supposed he really was. Because while he had come of age nearly two years ago, and while his body was formed and muscled enough that he had been able to help her father cut wood in the forest for the past three years, she couldn't help thinking that he was still – really – just a child, just like she was still a child, she supposed. Although the coming of her age was pregnant above her, although she could still feel her own age (*her womanhood*? an inner voice suggested uncertainly) bursting in on her so much it felt like drowning – she still felt, standing in this clearing, surrounded by all the townspeople – like not much more than a little girl.

Joseph had stopped speaking, and held his arms aloft in a silent salutation to the moon above. For what seemed like an impossibly long time, nothing happened. The townspeople glanced at one another, expectant, waiting. Helena reflected, once again, that she was the only one present who had never experienced this before, and she wondered if she would be able to cope once things started happening. The clearing was dull and gloomy now, lit only by a few torches. Somewhere in the distance, a bird called. Helena thought that it might be a sparrow. Right here, however, the clearing was deathly quiet. All the animals were staying well away. Finally, the clouds drew away from the moon, like a magician pulling back the silks on a final trick. Helena allowed herself to look up. The moon was a perfect disc of silver. Helena drew a breath in. To her, the shadows on the moon had always looked like a man's kindly smile. Tonight, it looked more like a sneer.

Her father was the first to change. There was a loud popping sound that made Helena think of the dry twigs that often snapped and cracked underfoot in the autumn months. That was her father's neck lengthening to at least three times its normal length. Bone and gristle stretched to accommodate the skull that was even now bulging outward, the ears flattening and becoming more pointed. Hair grew rapidly, so quickly in fact that it had its own sound – it sounded like it was punching its way out of her father's very flesh. Helena supposed that that was exactly what was happening. Another sound exploded from his throat, and Helena realised that her father was screaming in pain – or at least he would be, if his vocal cords would just stay in the same shape in order to accommodate such a task. There was a series of sounds that sounded like gunshots, and, as Helena watched, her father's haunches shot out, growing out at angles. He dropped to all fours, the muscles in his thighs bulging out and covered in coarse black hair that had not been there moments before: he had transformed from man to beast in less than a minute. Her eyes had been fixed on her father, but she did not need to look around to know that everyone else had also changed. The sounds all around her told her that much.

Helena stood there, chest heaving with what she had not yet identified as fear. One young, naked woman standing alone in a forest clearing, surrounded by at least ninety snarling, almost entirely non-sentient creatures. Their breathing, wetter and more ragged than hers. In a moment, she would have to run. She didn't dare chance a look at where Joseph stood. She had never seen him in wolf form before, and she did not want to start now. She had identified only one gap in the circle – mercifully very near to her – where she could have any hope of escape.

These creatures would certainly be able to run much faster than she could. And, as hardly needed pointing out (but her subconscious seemed determined to do anyway), there were very much more of them than there was of her. If she tripped, they would rip into her before she even hit the ground, whether they were her father, lover, or anyone else at all in the village.

She breathed in.

The wolves, as one, did the same.

She breathed out.

The wolves, as one, did the same.

She ran.

The wolves, as one, did the same.

*

Luck and chance saved her as much as anything else did. If she had planned her escape in any great detail, it would have been very likely that she would have ended up panicking at the myriad of chances that it had to fail. As it was, the plan she decided to go with consisted mainly of running. She pelted toward the only gap in the circle that was within her vision. This involved coming very close – far too close – to a wolf who in daylight hours was a young man called Oscar. Since Oscar in his human form had the challenge of being badly short-sighted (his glasses were neatly discarded at his feet, perched on his folded robes), Helena took the chance – a not entirely uneducated one – that Oscar's reflexes as a wolf would be roughly similar to how he might act while in human form.

As Helena ran to the gap next to Oscar, she suddenly switched direction. Not by much, but certainly by enough that, if she put enough force into it, she could clip Oscar on the shoulder as she passed by. If she got any closer to him, she ran the very real risk of simply running directly into his waiting claws. Too far away, and he would be able to lunge forward and catch her as she attempted to pass. However, she had judged it just right: as she ran past, she leaned into him, putting as much of her weight on him as she dared before she ran the risk of toppling over. It worked. Her shoulder slammed into his chest, and with a surprised, wide-eyed expression that closely resembled his human, bespectacled face, he topped backwards. She almost fell over him, but only stumbled, regained her footing, and with a leap over a tree stump, she escaped the clearing. It didn't sound like the rest of the wolves had even begun to chase her yet. She didn't risk looking back to check.

She didn't have any clear idea of where to run, so she ran forward. It did occur to her to zig-zag, to continually change her direction, but she thought that trick would not work with any of her pursuers. For one thing, there was a lot more of them than there was of her, and more than that: they had her scent. Joseph certainly did.

She ran without thinking. Abandoning thought was an actual, calculated choice: thought itself was pushed to the very back of her consciousness, her single focus on the route ahead, on her escape. In this, she was relentless and almost as animalistic as those who pursued her. She allowed her body to take over, her eyes seeking out the best route forward only seconds before her legs took the advice and carried her through a ragged gap in the trees. Branches lashed out at her as she stumbled past. She ignored the pain, not even allowing herself the grim pleasure of a wince. She imagined that she could hear the crashing through the trees of beasts only a few feet behind her. She pictured their claws just inches away from her bare spine. She ran on. She didn't have a chance to stop for over an hour.

*

Now, she sat comfortably on a heavy branch, which gave her a good vantage point. The wolves were circling below at the edge of the stream, confused. It was apparent they'd assumed that Helena would be in the water itself, and they were waiting for her to surface. She glanced down at her right hand, and despite the immediate danger, almost burst out laughing when she saw what was in her tight grasp. Somehow, despite her need to make a quick escape from the clearing, she had –

impossibly, it now seemed to her – found time to pick up her gown. At least you've got your priorities right, she thought to herself: modesty over personal safety.

She shrugged the gown over herself, and – despite the fact that there wasn't a human eye for miles to see her – immediately felt a lot better. She watched the wolves. It was clear that they were frustrated at not being able to catch their prey. She was tempted, despite the danger, to call out to them, but knew that she would have to wait until the following morning, when everyone was returned to their human form, to ask the question that was burning in her stomach: what had gone wrong with the ceremony? What was wrong with her? Why – alone amongst all the villagers – had she not Become?

As she watched, the wolves below began to shuffle off down the hill towards the forest. They had given up on finding Helena and they would need to hunt before morning returned. Helena waited a few minutes, and then carefully began to climb down the tree. There were tears prickling her eyes, and she fought them back. She began to walk back toward the village, for the first time in her life not at all certain that the village would want her amongst them.

*

Back home, she sat at the kitchen table, warming herself in front of the hearth, and waited for morning. Unlike the neighbouring villages in this part of the country, most did not felt the need to lock their doors on the night of a full moon. Most villagers were in the clearing in order to Become, and those that were not – the old or the infirm, looking after the children were comforted by the fact that the wolves never attacked the very young: in fact, it had always seemed impossible for wolves to even come within five feet of a child. She had hopelessly clutched at this fact already this morning – perhaps she herself was still too young? - but despaired: even if it was possible that everyone had somehow miscalculated her birthday, she doubted that they were seventeen years out.

It didn't take too long before her father, back in human form but still naked, returned. He nodded to her wordlessly as he fished some clothes out of the cupboard and pulled them on. He seemed unable to talk to her. Once he had dressed, however, he didn't immediately leave again as Helena had suspected – had been afraid – he would. So, he wasn't going to try to avoid her. Some things still need to be said. It just appeared that the conversation was not going to be started by him. He began to clatter various pots and pans around, in a great show of starting to prepare dinner. Since Helena's mother had died, her father liked to joke that thanks to his cooking, they would all be following her into the grave soon, but the fact was that he happened to be a very skilled cook.

She sat there, watching him slice and dice a vegetable that he couldn't quite identify, realising that the words were not coming easily to her, either. Finally, she decided to break the silence with the obvious question. 'What happened?'

Her father stopped what he was doing (he had begun to mess around with some pots on the stove, but had not actually started to use them in any real fashion). He turned to face her before sitting down at the kitchen table. 'I don't know,' he replied. 'It doesn't make any sense.' He stopped, although he must have known that what he'd just said could in no way be the end of the conversation. The silence spun out, through seconds into actual minutes. It hung above them until it began to feel like an actual thing, a physical presence.

She spoke again, this time through the sobs that were threatening to bubble up and overwhelm her. 'Daddy,' she said, 'What's wrong with me? Why didn't I Become?'

Her father didn't answer; he simply sat there, shaking his head slowly, unable to provide her with an answer. Equally, she was unable to stop herself from crying, not caring what she looked like, shame warming her cheeks. By now, she was certain, all of the townspeople – even the ones who had not been on the hilltop last night – would know that she had not changed, that the ceremony, in her case at least, had been a sham. The she had been blessed with the coincidence of her eighteenth birthday falling on the night of a full moon was supposed to have been cause for a particularly special celebration. The fact that her body had betrayed her and remained resolutely human would be the subject of speculation for years – perhaps even decades – to come, she was sure.

In an entirely rational and calm fashion, Helena began to consider the logistics of running away.

A new, disturbing thought came to her. 'Am I ... am I yours?' Her father looked at her in blank incomprehension for a few moments, clearly not understanding the question. She watched as he ran it through his head a couple of times, processing it and deciphering it. 'No,' he said at last. 'I mean, yes. Of course you're mine. You're my daughter. You're mine.' As he said this, with great authority, his face lapsed into an uneasy repose, as if he were considering for the very first time the possibility that his statement might be anything other than absolutely true.

'Tonight is full once more,' he said heavily. This was usually a statement of joy. At each full moon, and the nights on either side, the townspeople would turn into the pack. For three nights, they would hunt, taking the local wildlife – deer and such – which would provide food for the town for all of the following month. The moon loved them, and revealed where the deer hid. Indeed, it seemed the forest itself loved the pack as well, since the deer – and any other prey – would never venture far.

He told her in short, clipping sentences that she should stay home tonight, mentioning that it was probably best that she locked the doors: of course the wolves rarely came down here, but nothing like this had happened before, and if she was not a child, she was as vulnerable to attack as any wild animal. After these nights were over, he assured her, they would try to discover why she had not Become, and move on from there. While her father spoke, Helena said nothing. He gave her a gruff hug, and kissed her on the forehead. Helena managed to still her tears until after she left the kitchen, and got to her room.

*

Tonight, she had decided to stay in her room. She had avoided speaking to anyone else in the village all day. Certainly she had not wanted to see Joseph. It was likely that nobody would have anything to say to her. It was still possible of course that her failure to Become was merely the result of some unfortunate, overlooked, and most importantly, entirely innocent genetic quirk – but she was still unable to get past her paranoid conviction that she would be *judged*.

There was still light in the sky when she heard a knock at the door. She felt no fear; the moon had not yet risen, and the only people in town were the young and the very old who looked after them, and so she was surprised when she opened the door and saw Joseph standing there.

'You've got to leave,' she said urgently, glancing up at the sky. 'The moon will be out soon.' He was already shaking his head. 'I don't care,' he responded. 'I love you. I'd never hurt you.'

With a sigh, she placed a palm on his chest. Joseph was a very kind man, but he could often be impulsive. Even before last night, it had given her pause as to whether their relationship would continue for much longer after she Became. Now that it appeared she would not Become, she was beginning to worry that their relationship would survive even days. But right now, she was beginning to worry even more for her own safety. 'Once you're a wolf, you'll be an animal,' she warned. 'Get away from me. Please.'

He seemed to be about to argue, but clearly saw from her expression that she was not to be argued with. He leaned in and kissed her, and then stepped back. Helena closed the door on his departing back. By the time she got to her room, the moonlight was already streaming through the window. It was only when she heard the sound of splintering wood that she realised she had forgotten to lock the door.

*

Joseph – she could only think of him as Joseph, even when he was reduced to the snarling, drooling beast that now stood in front of her had arrived in her room two minutes ago – stood on his hind legs, and howled. His nostrils were flaring, and she wondered how much of her scent he could smell. They had only just kissed, after all.

'Joseph,' she said, calmly and steadily. 'I am Helena. You remember me. We have shared a bed. We *know* one another.' Joseph snarled, and took a few steps closer to her. She took a few steps back, her back pressing up against the wall. She had trapped herself. Joseph gave another snarl, and reached out a claw, seemingly to attack her, and then stopped.

Helena was not watching his claws, however. Her attention had been on his eyes, which had been full of confusion – and now, dawning understanding. A whimper escaped his drooling jaws. He dropped to all fours, and then scampered up to her. If his intention had still been to attack, he would not have been able to respond in time, but instead, he nuzzled her belly, dropped his head, and slunk out of the room. She watched him go, comprehension slowly dawning.

Wolves never attack the very young.

Wolves can't even come near the young.

She rested her hand on her belly, and looked out of the window.

She began to count in her head.

If the baby was born in the spring, Helena might become by the next harvest.

Uncertain of her calculations, she looked up at the moonlight.

The moon smiled down at her.

A WHISPER FROM ME TO YOU

Charlotte had to admit, it was a lovely thing.

When the Kindle had first been released (and, she realised now, she had always thought of it like that, with a capitalised *K*), she had resisted the idea of ever buying one for herself, because why would she ever want one? She loved books, real books, the smell of them, the touch of them. She would not, for instance, ever feel entirely comfortable reading an eBook in the bath (not that she believed that they contained enough power to ever be a danger, and in any case, didn't things have to be actually plugged in to cause you a problem?). She was, she'd argue, very much an old-fashioned girl.

She often read in the bath. This was the main point she would raise about traditional print books, the one that she would often produce against Kindles, only acutely aware that whenever she spoke about reading in the bath, it would elicit a bout of either distracted stammering or intense leering from whatever man she was speaking with (and let's face it, it was almost always a man who had chosen to pick this argument with her). The leering was obviously tiresome, although she could sometimes see that the stammering was probably quite sweet, even if it served no practical purpose.

So, yes, it was more often men than women with whom she had this conversation: books or eBooks? It was weird enough, she had often reflected, that she had found herself in the conversation so often that she was able to track it in terms of demographics. Just because these men were well read and apparently intelligent, that apparently gave them the right to begin the argument (and in all honesty, it always ended up being an argument, rather than a conversation) on their terms, nobody else's.

It's my way or you're wrong.

As soon as these men had worked out that she was a reader – not exactly a difficult thing to discover, in all fairness, since she was often to be seen with a battered paperback in one hand, the other hand gently tapping her coffee cup and (although she didn't know this last, since nobody had ever pointed it out to her), an eyebrow darting up and down as she lost herself in the lives of the characters she was reading about.

She could read anywhere, so much so that she was often honestly confused by anyone else who wasn't reading all the time – in a queue waiting for the bus, in the park on her lunchbreak, even during the interval at a show if she'd gone on her own – and, obviously, in a coffee shop. It was the coffee shops where she got the most unasked for attention.

The men, usually broad and loud and earning at least three times more than she ever would (she knew this because the details of their salary was something that was somehow very swiftly dropped into conversation) usually marked their territory early on by positioning on the table (her table) the latest version of the latest phone where she couldn't fail to see it.

Charlotte wasn't exactly a luddite – she was as much a sucker for a cool new piece of tech as anyone else – but such conversational gambits bored her to the point of bewilderment. Often when these guys saw her reading a paperback, they would feel compelled to tell her (because apparently the very fact of her trying to read a book wasn't enough of a clue that she might want not to be disturbed) that eBooks were the future, that print was dead. That was the problem, Charlotte had eventually decided but rarely bothered to say: she had read about enough different versions of the future to know that it wasn't always a particularly welcoming place.

She was, of course, in a future right now. Uncharted territory. Last year, her bed had seemed too small, the coldness radiating from Isobel as her bare back was her only companionship each evening. Even now, Charlotte refused to accept (all of) the blame for the collapse of their relationship, but she would still occasionally catch herself wondering if there was something she could have done differently.

Perhaps, she considered, the split was one of the reasons why she was currently reading so voraciously. But that was a cheap answer; a distraction. The truth was that she (and Izzie, come to that) had always read tons of books – in fact, Charlotte still had lots of Izzie's books still at the flat – and far from being the thing she was losing herself in these days, the books were, if not precisely a salvation, then certainly a salve.

However, her mother had bought her a kindle (still at that point named in her mind with a small *K*) for her last birthday. Presumably she knew it was the one thing that Charlotte did not already have. It had seemed wrong – selfish, even – not to have accepted the gift gratefully. Charlotte and her mother had never had that much in common, and the space between them grew wider each year with a speed that was terrifying. Charlotte supposed that within a few years – perhaps as few as twenty, which did not seem as long a time as it once had – her mother would be gone.

She – Charlotte – had often thought that of her mother dropped dead today (whenever 'today' happened to be), it wouldn't really upset or even affect her. But equally, it was possible that when her mother did die, she would be entirely unprepared for it. And the Kindle at least suggested that her mother knew she liked to read, and there had been times in her life when she didn't feel that her mother knew even that much about her life.

When she opened the box containing the Kindle, she spent the first few hours doing what – she imagined – pretty much everybody else did: she downloaded all the free classics. On went the Austen, the Dickens, and the Brontës. She also found a relatively obscure Wollstonecraft, an annotated edition for which she had already forked out thirty quid when buying the physical edition a couple of years previously. On it went.

Having the eBook had not stopped her buying physical books, of course. In fact, it was very possible that she had bought more printed books since having the Kindle than she had in the whole of the previous year. She thought, cheerfully, that she now possessed more books than she ever had any reasonable chance of ever managing to read within her lifetime. The whole of their (sorry, her, just the one of them now, Isobel was back in York) living room wall was given over to bookcases – all overstuffed and mismatching. She and Isobel had had to spend an entire evening last winter bolting all the bookcases together so that each supported the other. They had briefly considered bolting the bookcases directly into the wall itself, but as Isobel had pointed out, that was exactly the kind of behaviour that was likely to lose them their deposit.

Ironically, the device really came into its own – for Charlotte, at least – by delivering to her (for a price) the kinds of things she might not normally have paid for. There were a fair few newspapers that had kindle editions, and they arrived each morning on her device without her having to walk down to the newsagent in the cold. She couldn't help but feel some small, nagging feeling of disquiet. After all, her local newsagent was one of the last few remaining, replaced by the likes of a Tesco Metro. The beginnings of the end of human interaction.

There were also the blogs. As someone who had taken a journalism degree when she was younger (and look where *that* had got her), she had started writing her own blog, and like many people who had started writing a blog, she had entirely failed to keep up with it. Nonetheless, the idea of blogging itself still fascinated her. The early days – the time when it was still theoretically possible for someone to make some money out of an online diary – had long passed into history (for those people, the business had migrated onto YouTube), but there were still many thousands – millions, perhaps – of people all across the planet sharing their thoughts with passing strangers.

As far as she understood it, there were certain blogs that you could pay for, thus supporting the writer, and each blog that would be delivered just as often as the writer uploaded an entry. The entries could be found in the usual way, via browsing the web, but she thought this might be a neat way to have all the blogs she liked to hand. As long as she could find a few blogs she actually liked.

She typed a couple of words into the search engine. *Blog. Brighton.* Then, as an afterthought, as a salute to her current location: *coffee.*

In response, the details for eight blogs came up, most of them apparently written by someone who had absolutely no intention of adding to their readership. The last time the most recently updated of them had a fresh entry was over nine months ago. Two of them were about coffee shops in a completely different Brighton (not in the UK). Another seemed like it was a work of fiction.

However, second from the top of the list was a blog that caught her eye: *Views From A (Brighton) Bridge.* The café that Charlotte was sat in now was called The Bridge, a somewhat incongruous name since it was nowhere near any bridge or indeed any water feature that might at any point have required a bridge. But Charlotte thought that it was at least likely that it was this café that the blog was making reference to, even if you ignored the fact that the blog name was a weak allusion to the title of an old Arthur Miller play. Perhaps more importantly, she saw now, was that this blog had actually been updated less than ten hours ago. How had she missed that? Checking the details over, she learned that the writer of the blog claimed to update posts daily and that – yes - each post could be delivered automatically to her kindle.

The idea pleased her: that someone could send to her their thoughts and musings each morning for her to read, which then might prompt her to have thoughts and musings of her own. Apparently the writer of this blog lived in the same city as she did (perhaps even the same neighbourhood, if the name of the blog was to be taken at face value), which made things even more intriguing. She clicked on the link.

Below the payment details, a single line in Amazon's simple typeface: *Your blog will be delivered to you via Whispernet.*

Whispernet. Charlotte's eyebrow arched again. She was entirely unaware that at least eight women (and half as many men, for that matter) had fallen in love with her almost entirely as a result of being initially distracted by that eyebrow. *Whispernet.* What an odd name. Even an ugly one. It sounded like...

She stopped to think, the arched eyebrow collapsing into a frown. What *did* it sound like? The eyebrow popped up again. Like heavy cobwebs, she decided. She tapped in a few more words, all the while glancing back at the screen of her Kindle, grey and impassive.

A moment, and the screen blanked out (*the dead cobwebs are visiting,* she thought randomly, before wondering if that was a phrase she could use somewhere eventually) and then announced the arrival of her purchase: *NEW – VIEWS FROM A BRIGHTON BRIDGE.*

Below the title, today's date, and then:

Today has been a better day. There were a lot of tourists in town, and unlike a lot of the locals I speak to, I actually like the tourists.

She scanned down a few entries, and found this:

The g/f still isn't talking to me. I may have to play nice.

She scowled. Maybe she should have read this before paid for it. She scanned a few more entries, but couldn't see anything else to disquiet her, and in any case, people were allowed to bitch about their partners, weren't they? She of all people knew that.

Nonetheless, she didn't much feel like reading the blog any more. She put the Kindle away, and paid for her coffee.

She didn't go back to The Bridge for a couple of days.

*

The café was pretty typical for the area; and appeared to have actual shifts throughout the day where different blocks of character types would make way for one another. In the mornings, it was full of what everyone – still – referred to as 'yummy mummies' – impossibly attractive young women with heartbreakingly beautiful babies. If ever an advertising executive found themselves in here just before lunch, they would find most of their work done for them.

After lunch, of course, it was the locals who seemed to treat this place as an extension of their own office. These were the guys (and again, it was usually men; if women did the same, she hadn't really noticed) who spread their possessions over an entire table, plugged their laptop into a power point, and made a habit of chatting (flirting with) the girl behind the counter as she tried to serve someone else. The girl behind the counter – a cute punk with more metal in her face than Charlotte would have thought was allowed in an establishment that sold food – was very good at smiling brightly, and seeming fascinated by Loud Man's brashness and storytelling. Perhaps she really was fascinated, Charlotte had to remind herself. It had been a long time since she herself had been in a position to read the signals.

Being back at The Bridge reminded her that she hadn't looked at the blog in the last couple of days. So much for paying out for daily deliveries.

People don't look around at their surroundings. They spend too much time gazing at their screens, and where does that information get them?

Charlotte felt a little irritated, and she couldn't quite define if her reaction was unreasonable or not. It was a bit rich, wasn't it, for this blogger, whoever he was, to moan about people spending too much time looking at their screens if the medium via which he was choosing to complain was .. a blog?

Today's date.

I think I've seen the replacement for the g/f. Cute. Nice hair. Always reading. She hasn't been in for the last few days, but she's back.

Two things too far too long to occur to her. The second came to her while she was still absorbing the first. The blog was describing her. She read it a couple of times to confirm, each subsequent time wondering how she could have missed it the first time, it was so obvious. Fear, ice in her stomach, was just about held at bay. But it would come.

The second realisation was two-fold. The word *here*. And the time. He'd posted the entry just five minutes ago. He was still here.

She glanced around the coffee shop, as calmly as she was able. Her attention was focussed on the people hunched over their laptops, which was why she didn't pay much attention to the scrawny boyish figure sat near the door, who had seemingly spent the last hour scrolling on his phone. It simply never occurred to Charlotte that one could update a blog directly from their phone.

The way she understood it. From everything she had read, you couldn't send a blog directly and exclusively to a Kindle (*other eBooks are available*, she thought) – the blog entry would still be posted on the website, and from that, then be updated on the Kindle. She looked online for the original blog, but could not find it. No clue as to who had originally written this blog entry that apparently described her.

She peered at the blog entry on her kindle, and copied a line from it into the search engine on her laptop. Not long before the results threw up a whole lot of suggestions, but not one of them the blog she was looking for, even though she could see it right there, on her own Kindle. It was as if the blog entry was just for her. She looked around the café again, and – hating herself for the small tangle of panic that was beginning to unravel in her belly – decided that she would feel better if she got out of here. She paid for her coffee, and left.

The scrawny boy left a couple of minutes later.

Charlotte's flat wasn't far from the café – Isobel and she had always said that they were 'going downstairs' when they meant going for a coffee – and it didn't take her long to get back. Her block of flats was a smart, tall building, and Charlotte had always been grateful that she lived on the ground floor. If nothing else, it meant that she was one of only six tenants – out of ninety – that had a garden.

The guy darted in front of her and reached the door before she did. He glanced up at her with a passing distracted interest as he fished in his pocket for his keys. This was always a somewhat awkward moment, to be confronted with a neighbour that you didn't quite recognise (although this one was pretty familiar; she was fairly certain she had seen him at least once already this morning) who was coming through the entrance at the same time as you. There was an unwritten rule in this block of facts (actually, it was written – typed, in fact, but the piece of paper, once tacked to the wall in the hallway had been long since lost) – you didn't let *anyone* in who didn't have a key of their own, no matter who they were, no matter who they said they knew, what flat they claimed to live in. So Charlotte had to go through the pointless rigmarole of retrieving her own keys, despite the certainty that this guy would beat her to it, and end up holding the door open for her. Later, she would hate herself for not spotting the very obvious.

*

An hour later, as she lay on her own kitchen floor with her lip bleeding, Charlotte was silently screaming at herself for her own stupidity: *you knew what he was. You knew he was tricking you.*

That was easy enough to say now. But when that moment had come, it was so banal, so normal, she had dismissed it, despite her earlier freak-out about the blog entry. As the man outside the door had patted his pockets for the last time and given her a half-hearted apology for not being able to find his keys more quickly, she thought – quite coldly and rationally – that he was probably lying, that he was play-acting so that he could push in once she had unlocked the door with her own keys.

She thought of all of this, but still reached for her keys, she still reached past him to open the door. For a brief moment, her fist even formed around the keys themselves so that she could clutch them in between her fingers, as she had heard (where from, she no longer remembered) that doing so would be a good form of protection. But, feeling vaguely embarrassed (God, was that all it was? Getting attacked or robbed or raped just because you were fucking *embarrassed*?), she had pushed all those feelings aside and unlocked the door anyway. She approached her own front door, even glancing back to see if he was following her or getting into the lift and seeing nothing before finally relaxing.

When the man pushed into her – and he really did push all of his weight into her, like some kind of embrace – it was both unsurprising and terrifying. A blackly banal phrase bubbled up – *so it's my turn now* – as she stumbled back. Her panic lasted less than two seconds, and then she pushed back, aware that there was nothing behind her but an enclosed space. She was going to scratch, hit and punch him. Perhaps because she was attempting to conserve her energy, she forgot to yell or scream. That was another thing she berated herself while lying on her kitchen floor.

He had stumbled back slightly as she pushed back, and with no ceremony or even evident pleasure, swung a fist to her jaw. He wasn't taking any chances, and he wanted her unconscious as quickly as possible. Another banal phrase: *you've done this before*, and then blackness swallowed her.

When she regained consciousness, her jaw was screaming pain at her, feeling like metal scraping against metal. She was lying down on her own kitchen floor. He had used her own keys to get into her flat. She shifted her weight (her back felt like there were small, splintered pieces of wood stuck in there), and he snapped, 'Don't move.' She complied, but watched him carefully. He hadn't tied her up, and weirdly, the fact that she was in her own kitchen provided her with – was that hope? Strength? *You're fighting on your home turf,* a voice comforted her, and she was delighted to realise that the voice was her own.

'I need to sit up. And lean against something. I've got a bad back.'

He considered this for a moment, and then gestured to the front room. It was very clear that his hand that was doing the gesturing gripped a very large knife. 'Move. Now. Don't try anything, or I'll ..'

Charlotte did as she was told, musing that he hadn't quite been able to vocalise violence even while threatening it. She sat down on the floor, and leaned heavily against the bookcase.

See? Books will protect you. EBooks are nothing but trouble.

Her jaw was still complaining, and she let her head hang loose. This shelf actually had relatively few books on it, just a couple of graphic novels, and a small statue of the Wicked Witch Of The West that Isobel had bought her for Christmas a few years back. She looked in the eyes of the witch, trying to regulate her breathing. She was slightly startled when the man's hand came into her line of vision, and took the statue off the shelf. Perhaps he had thought she was going to try and throw it at him.

She shifted her weight again, dropping her arm on the now mostly empty shelf to support her. He seemed excited, but relaxed. That worried her. He looked happy to take his time, and wasn't worried about the fact that she had seen his face.

He disappeared to the kitchen, and Charlotte could hear clattering sounds, almost as if he had dropped the knife in her sink.

She had not heard of any attacks by strangers in women's own homes.

He came back in. He was pulling his shirt off. He looked strong and happy.

There would be no signs of forced entry. Nobody had seen either of them come in. She wondered how many attacks, how many

say it

how many rapes and murders had happened and the official line was that the victims had let him into their homes.

How many he had talked about on his blog?

How many times he had done this before?

'They're going to find you, you know,' she said, and had not been entirely sure that she was going to be speaking until after the words were already coming out of her mouth, 'if you're going to be such a fucking idiot that you write about your next victim in your blog.' Another thought occurred to her. In the scheme of things, it didn't matter as much, but it unaccountably made her angry. Her hand gripped tightly onto the back of the shelf. 'And we're not your girlfriends, or your "G F"s.' That said, she dropped her head again. Being captured in your own home was strangely exhausting. When he didn't say anything in response, she looked up at him. Bizarrely, he was blushing.

'You've read my blog? That is so cool. I don't have any subscribers.'

Charlotte bit her tongue, in actuality as well as metaphor. She couldn't quite believe what he'd just suggested: that all of this was a coincidence, that the one blog she happened to subscribe to was written by the man who then attacked her – and it was all just happenstance.

She smiled to herself. *Happenstance.* One of Isobel's favourite words. Might have even been the title of one of her books. Charlotte would have to read it one day, if she could find it.

He saw her smile, and gave her a smile back, a smile that was genuinely attractive. He walked closer to her, and stopped, standing over her. She thought about kicking up at him, but knew even without moving that the pain in her back would stop her doing any damage. 'I'm glad you've decided to enjoy it,' he said, genially. 'It's no fun for me if it's no fun for you.'

You fucking liar

He began to crouch down to her, and she gripped the shelf even tighter, marvelling that her arms seemed to be the only part of her that wasn't screaming in pain.

He began to speak. He was telling her to do something. His voice seemed very far away.

She tensed her arm.

And *pulled.*

Each of the eight bookcases in her room contained around seventy books each. She and Isobel shared an incurable love of hardbacks. The weight of just one bookcase would be enough to surprise anyone.

And Charlotte and Isobel had spent an entire evening bolting them all together.

As soon as Charlotte felt the bookcase begin to shift towards her, she rolled away from it (and *him*). He glanced up in confusion, and managed to react pretty quickly, rolling away also.

To where all the other bookcases were now following suit, like a house of cards or a stack of dominoes.

He sputtered something, and put up a hand to stop the fall of the bookcase. Charlotte couldn't see what happened next, but a very clear splintering sound and a scream gave her a pretty good idea. She shifted her weight once more, to get away from what was now a massive pile of books, wood, and one buried rapist in the middle of her room. His muffled screams and shouting were getting increasingly more frantic. She got to her feet, keeping a wary eye on the place where he had fallen. She had seen enough horror movies to not want to turn her back.

She left the flat, and leaned on the door. She took her phone out of her pocket (incredibly, he hadn't taken it from her), and tapped a single number, three times.

They told her they'd be there in less than five minutes.

She allowed herself to sink to the floor, still leaning on the door.

She had no concerns about leaving him in there until the police arrived. She was just annoyed that she had nothing to read while she waited.

BROOM HANDLE

Arnold Six parked his car, noting as he did so that the readout on his windscreen display told him that it was exactly two minutes to eleven. That was good: that gave him less than ten minutes before he was due for today's Op, and if he had had to hang around waiting for too long, he might just turn around and run, delaying things yet again, and that would be a bad idea. He couldn't really delay the Op any longer than he already had, as much as he wanted to.

In fact, he probably wouldn't even have made it this far today if he hadn't allowed his mother to persuade him. But then, his mother had always been a very persuasive woman. He had visited her earlier this morning simply because of her gentle, firm, and often repeated hints that he had not done so in a very long time, and he supposed the accusation was true. He hadn't seen her in almost a year, and since her apartment was less than five minutes from the Op Centre, he had to concede that he really didn't have much of an excuse this time.

He supposed he was something of a bad son, really. He always tried to claim that he was often too busy to visit as much as he wanted, but that was a weak excuse, and he suspected they both knew it. He had decided – particularly ever since today's Op had become pretty much inevitable – that he was going to make much more of an effort to see his mother regularly. After all, as she had pointed out to him (gently, firmly, repeatedly) she wasn't going to be around forever: she was over two hundred years old.

When he had arrived at her apartment that morning, she was already waiting for him in her doorway. He was glad about that: the main door led to the hallway which then led on to various apartments, and he could not honestly remember which one was hers (*bad son, bad son*) and if she hadn't called to him in greeting, he would have utterly failed to recognise her.

It was a sign, if one had been needed, that her last round of Ops had been a complete success. His mother (who was currently named Alice Seventeen) embraced him tightly before inviting him in. He estimated that she had likely clocked at least six Ops since they had last seen one another. No wonder that he was worried about recognising her. Fortunately, she always uploaded photos to update everybody after each successive (and successful) Op. This she did freely and happily: she was understandably delighted when an Op made her look younger than her years (this was not always guaranteed, not even at her age). This was one of the strangest unexpected side effects of the Ops, a process the system's originators had always claimed was entirely democratic. The system had the random beauty of a roulette wheel, meaning that Arnold's mother, twenty years his senior, now looked at least forty years younger.

Arnold had heard that uploading post-Op pictures was going to be made compulsory, perhaps as soon as the next election. It answered the concern that the right had been voicing more in recent years: nowadays, the average Citizen might have as many as fifteen separate Ops over the course of ten years, and it was certainly possible to have at least six different faces in one lifetime. This led to hotly debated arguments about identity, and certain criminal elements attempting to escape justice, but despite all this, Arnold did not himself believe that Citizens would be legally compelled to upload images of every new face for at least a couple of years: there were now much easier ways to identify people than simply what someone looked like, which was becoming less relevant with every passing year.

Fingerprints also meant nothing, he considered, flexing his hand. There were plenty of other things that told you all you needed to know about a person's identity, he thought. So many changes.

Oddly enough, the change about his mother that struck Arnold was her new hairstyle, which was now a black, shiny and sharply cut bob. Ridiculous, really. The hairstyle was in no way the most significant change in his mother: it was the face that the hairstyle framed. It was a face that – if he had judged correctly – was at least forty years younger than the one he currently wore.

His mother took a while to release him, and if anything, her embrace become ever tighter the longer it continued. That was understandable considering how long it had been since they had last seen one another, but Arnold was still unable to stop himself shifting uncomfortably until finally she released him and said 'You'd better go in.' He noticed that she avoided her usual affectionate habit of tightly gripping his arm, for which he was profoundly grateful.

'Let me look at you,' she said when they were both inside. Arnold stepped back from her with a slightly uneasy feeling of disbelief – he was only now truly understanding that as well as his mother having gone through several Ops since the last time they had seen one another, he too would look completely different to her, as well. 'Such a handsome face,' she said, touching his cheek lightly with her hand, before bustling into the hallway, taking his coat. Arnold couldn't help but feel absurdly pleased: he had secretly allowed himself to think that his latest face was a good one, but he hadn't been entirely sure.

For one thing, the skin colouring on his (new) face didn't match the rest of his body, not even his neck. That sort of thing was to be expected, of course – it happened all the time. Citizens had long ago accepted such disparities as an entirely normal – even mundane – part of the process. Occasionally- even these days! – one heard stories about a Citizen refusing a replacement body part just because it was a significantly different colour to the rest of them. This was quite a rare occurrence now, and such Citizens were routinely derided for their naiveté and bigotry. They ended up as the amusing 'and finally' reports at the end of news broadcasts.

It could perhaps be argued that Arnold had been slightly unlucky with last three Ops (if you chose to describe any Op as being unlucky, which nobody did): the last few limbs he had Inherited had all come from Citizens older than him. And while Arnold still looked much younger than his Core Age – 171 next birthday – any casual observer who saw the two of them next to one another would peg him as older than his own mother. The chance of them standing next to one another, as his mother would doubtless take glee in pointing out – would be a fine thing, given how rarely he chose to visit.

Many Citizens had acknowledged long ago that the head (and most of its contents) aged more quickly than most other parts of the human body. Arnold was now on his sixth head, a balding dome that compensated for its criss-cross of wrinkles (and lack of hair) by being cheerfully good looking.

Arnold waited patiently as his mother took in his new face, noting with some sadness that her eyes had finally been replaced. She had managed to keep the same pair for just over a hundred years – quite an impressive length of time by anyone's standards – and he had come to think of the wide, chocolatey eyes as essentially *hers* – her own – in as much as any body part could be said to truly belong to any Citizen.

It had been established very early on that Citizens would never be able to bid on particular body parts to suit whatever idealised version they had of themselves. The whole concept, the very idea of simply swapping complicated surgical procedures and care with replacing one body part with another when old age or disease ravaged them had been more positively embraced by Citizens than had been expected or even dared hoped. Of course, there had been concern voiced in The City (Arnold knew this because he had still been working there at the time, back when he still had a surname rather than a number) that the public, encouraged by a ghoulish, negatively minded media, would pass on dark, paranoid mutterings about 'body farming', and 'harvesting' and the like.

The response from the health officials was clear-eyed, but no less surprising for all that: yes, it *was* body farming. That was the only way the human race was going to survive the next 100 years, what with a new virus or disease ripping through the population every couple of months, it seemed. And there were still thousands – millions – of people dying daily, and they were leaving behind perfectly good body parts. It was not good to be wasteful these days. It was certainly true in the early years (before Arnold had even been born) that there had been much discussion and argument debating whether or not the method of Replacement Ops was a more viable (in other words: cheaper) process than hospital care and surgery, or if it was in fact more wasteful. Over the following decades, the former was proven to be true: previously, many billions of dollars had been ploughed into what were now considered ultimately wasteful and even futile procedures. Arnold hadn't met anyone who quite understood the science, but it was now accepted by most that this seemingly more 'butcher slab' approach – *cut it off and replace it with another* – was now the way of things.

*

Arnold walked through the entrance to the clinic, pausing the customary few moments as the sensors picked up on his details. It was at times like this that he imagined he could sense the implant pulse inside him as it sent out its information. He was holding his left hand tightly with the forefinger and thumb of his right. It seemed that the old cliché of aches and pains acting up in damp weather was absolutely true. The receptionist looked up at him as her display pad beeped merrily at her. 'Good morning, Arnold 143,' she said, motioning to an empty seat. 'Doctor Sinesh is running a little late this morning.' Arnold grunted in reply, not quite trusting himself to speak. For a moment, he considered simply walking straight back out of the door again, before remembering that his arrival had already been logged by the computer. He slumped down in the chair, and waited.

He glanced around at the posters and pamphlets that were scattered around the reception, wondering idly why (as he always did at this point) the clinics still provided information on paper paraphernalia rather than on screens. And then (as he always did at this point), he provided his own answer: he imagined it gave people a sense of nostalgic security, of being *safe*, a sense that – no matter what modern procedure they were submitting themselves to, they were doing it in an environment that stated clearly and compassionately: *this is how we did it in the good old days*.

People might require as many as six Ops in a single year, replacing parts of themselves as easily as getting upgrades on their phone, kaleidoscoping their way through innumerable body parts in one lifetime. Ops had been commonplace since long before Arnold was born, but even now there was the palpable sense of wonder that the science existed at all, a feeling that humans were in some way touching immortality. They weren't, of course: while Citizen's lifespans had been greatly increased, death itself was still as commonplace as ever: undetected diseases still claimed millions, as did sudden and unexpected death – if somebody found themselves on the wrong side of a gun or a speeding car, then it would be all over for them even with the swiftest emergency Op. And then of course there were the Citizens who, after several decades of having body parts replaced to lengthen their lives, voluntarily elected for Closure.

Closure had been his mother's main concern when they had met this morning. He had mentioned, oh so casually, that he was considering postponing his Op. He chose not to remind her that if he did, it would be for the third time.

'Are you saying goodbye, Arnold?' his mother had asked, her voice catching slightly on his name. It was the first time it had even occurred to him of how his decision might come across to somebody else. 'God, no,' he had replied quickly. 'I'm not going anywhere, anytime soon. No – I want to live, no question.' And on that, his mother visibly relaxed, a huge smile breaking over her (brand new) features.

Arnold found himself considering what he had told her – *I feel better than I have in years*. Well, that wasn't strictly true, was it? Hence today's Op. He had been in pain for quite some time now, and while painkillers managed to alleviate the worst of it, such items were becoming increasingly difficult to obtain, not just because they were expensive, but also because they were being made in far fewer quantities these days: there was much less use for them.

*

Now, Arnold was sitting in the chair, waiting for the doctor to finish perusing her notes. 'You're an interesting case,' she told him. Doctor Sinesh was a handsome Asian woman who currently had her back to him as she looked through his file, digitally projected onto the wall. It had kicked into life as soon as he had entered the room. He had sat down, noting without much surprise a small blue ring on Doctor Sinesh's thumb, indicating that she was an Alpha – fully original, no parts yet replaced. He would probably have been able to guess as much anyway, since she was still operating under a birth name as opposed to a number (although such names could still be purchased for obscene amounts of money), and she had no mismatches in her skin colour. None that he could see, anyway.

The regulations on Alphas were very strict, meaning that even if someone had an Op as simple as correcting their vision, it would mean that the Citizen in question could no longer qualify as 'original'. There had been a time, back when Arnold was still a child, when Alphas had still been referred to as 'pure,' but that had been dismissed as needlessly combative and emotive language. There was always a huge demand for Alphas in the sex industry. Arnold glanced at Doctor Sinesh, noting the way her blouse was buttoned, the pale blue of the cotton contrasting with the darkness of her skin. He glanced up, finally seeing that she had seen him looking. He blushed. There might have been a passing twitch at her mouth, but otherwise there was no other response.

'I note that you're in a great deal of pain with your left hand,' she murmured. Her voice had become softer. Arnold suspected that this was the tone she adopted when telling people the News They Did Not Want To Hear. That they were untreatable, perhaps. That their body would finally lose at the roulette table, and reject a replacement limb. She indicated his left hand with her own, almost as if she was concerned that he would not know what she was talking about.

Deciding that there was no way to broach the subject gently, he jumped right in. 'Is there ... is there any way we could *not* replace this hand? That we could treat it instead?' Doctor Sinesh's brow creased in confusion, although Arnold was reasonably confident that she must have heard this pathetic plea – or at least some version of it – many times before. The confusion was surely pantomimed for his benefit. She walked around her desk to meet him. An elegant and simple black skirt ending just at her knees. She perched herself on the desk, and took his hand in hers. Her manner was entirely professional, although still his breath caught in his throat. Her slim hands felt cool against his.

'This hand is now very old,' she told him gently. 'It's no longer fit for purpose. Look, you're not even fully in control.' She scooped her own palm upwards, allowing his hand to rest on hers, where it shook like a dazed butterfly contemplating flight. Arnold tried to tell himself that his hand was quivering simply because he was so unused to a beautiful young woman holding it, but even unvoiced, he dismissed the idea as the lie it obviously was even before it was half formed in his mind.

She arched an eyebrow at him, and he took that as is cue that he should speak once more. Make his pitch. 'This hand ... is mine.' Doctor Sinesh frowned at him again, and this time, he had the impression that her confusion was genuine. 'I don't want this to go,' he said, shaking his hand at her for emphasis, and also to show that he was still in control of his hand, no matter what she thought. The pain made him involuntarily hiss, baring his teeth.

'I think you're being overly emotional, and certainly irrational,' Doctor Sinesh said firmly. 'That hand is no more 'you' than any other part of you. Your files tell me that you've had sixteen heart replacements. That's quite a lot for not even 200 years. You've been through four brain

Ops. What makes that hand any more the original Arnold than anything else we've replaced many times over?'

Arnold didn't have an answer. Not a logical one, anyway. He knew that the brain he had been born with and had lain reasonably undisturbed inside his skull for the first ninety years of his life had long ago been sliced up and used for experiments in cell regeneration. His second brain had only lasted two years before succumbing very suddenly to dementia. That one had been incinerated in a hospital furnace in Milan. He knew that with each subsequent brain Op, his memories, his thoughts, everything that was *him* – were saved and uploaded to the replacement brain and cerebral cortex. He knew, logically, that every brain and heart he had ever Inherited was nothing other than a replacement organ or muscle with no soul or romance attached to it. He knew all of this. He knew very well what Doctor Sinesh was trying to make him understand. Knowing didn't make any difference, however. This hand was the very last part of him, the real him. He simply did not want to let it go.

How could she ever understand? She wasn't even forty, surely. How could she ever comprehend that this scar here, just under the thumb, was a souvenir from a pet dog when he was just six years old? That was almost two centuries ago. He retained almost no other memories from that period of his life – how could he? – but a passing glance at that fold of skin was enough to instantly transport him to a humid but drizzly day of his childhood. How could be tell Doctor Sinesh about this pale band of skin on his finger, where for sixty years a wedding ring had resided?

He began to cry. He didn't want to – he'd already noticed the box of tissues on her desk, and he suspected that she saw this kind of thing far too often to have any real sympathy for him – but the tears fell from his eyes anyway. Not, he thought with more than a touch of bitterness, that they were his eyes anyway. He'd seen the Inheritance Details. He – Arnold – had Inherited these eyes from a biker who had lost control in a rainstorm. In turn, the biker had inherited the eyes in the first place from a thirteen year old girl. Arnold continued to cry, realising for the first time in seventy years that he'd never learned the cause of the girl's death, or even her name.

'If I ... lose this hand,' – he licked his lips, not certain of what he was going to say next – 'it will be liked I've died. This is the last part of me. The last real part of me. After that, I'm just a stitched together bundle of corpses.' He looked back up at her, seeing that she was already preparing to speak. Of course, there was nothing original in what he had said to her; doubtless she had heard some version of it many times before. She was surely well trained to respond calmly and efficiently to whatever hysterics Citizens could throw at her. There was, he thought bitterly, nothing original about him whatsoever.

So he let her speak. He let her speak with her youth, her beauty, the arrogance of her childishness. Arnold hated her. He looked up at her again. She had stopped speaking. She was waiting for him to answer. He sat there, quite unable to get a single coherent thought through his head. He looked down at his left hand, which ironically, for the moment, seemed for the very first time in a long while to be causing him no discomfort whatsoever. He sighed. It was no good, Doctor Sinesh was right: he was being overly emotional. He looked up again. She was still waiting. He nodded slowly. 'Alright then,' he said finally, heavily. He proffered his hand. He looked, he thought crazily, like a hopeful suitor. 'Take my hand.'

*

The Op lasted sixteen minutes, which even for a simple procedure like a replacement hand was very swift. Citizens received Credits for each full hour that an Op took, and Arnold calculated ruefully that this particular Op would end up costing him Credits.

He blinked a few times, attempting to acclimatise himself. He had always found Op Wakes difficult. Doctor Sinesh was tapping a few details onto her screen, which now blinked its pale blue light, indicating her patient's wakefulness. She turned and smiled at him. It was the first time he had seen a real – genuine – smile from her. Something at the back of his head rumbled that if he had known about that smile earlier, he would have cheerfully thrown his hand away years ago. He pushed that thought away as she addressed him. 'How are we feeling?'

Arnold leaned back in his chair, honestly considering the question. 'I feel ... good,' he replied. He looked down. The hand that now sprung from his cuff was a similar age to the one that had caused him so much pain this morning. It even had the same clustering of liver spots he had become accustomed to seeing on his own hand. He flexed it tentatively a few times, and almost involuntarily something that was not quite a gasp fell from his mouth. There was no pain. It felt – and he almost laughed out loud at the stupidity of the phrase – like a brand new hand. He flexed it again, noting once more that whatever else it was, the hand was not young. Apart from the liver spots, it was deeply lined, and the colouring was not the ruddy pink of someone in their youth. In fact, apart from a small pink section on the ring finger, you could almost argue that this hand was grey. Arnold blinked, looking harder at the ring finger. He was not aware that he was holding his breath, not aware that Doctor Sinesh was watching him.

Slowly, he turned his hand over. Like the 'X' marking the spot on a treasure map, there was a slight, almost invisible scar, a souvenir from an overly excited puppy nearly two hundred years ago. He didn't dare look at Doctor Sinesh. His eyes were brimming with tears again. The image of his hand doubled, tripled, and then became indistinct.

'You're reaching your 200,' Doctor Sinesh was saying. 'Even if we up your visits to every two months, it's reasonable to assume you'll receive Closure in the next hundred years or so. Frankly, considering the condition of the last couple of hearts you've Inherited, it's a surprise it hasn't happened already. So it seems that, with the best will in the world, it won't be too long before we have to say goodbye to Arnold Six anyway. So, I thought... what's the harm?'

Arnold was unable to speak for a good few minutes. Doctor Sinesh waited. She appeared to be very good at waiting. Finally, he was able to voice his primary concern: 'You ... you won't be in any trouble, will you?' In response, her mouth twitched slightly again. 'It's possible that they'll call me into some training sessions where I'm reminded to keep my patient's best interests at heart,' she informed him, 'but what we've done today isn't exactly against the rules. Not yet, anyway.'

'Thank you. Thank you so much.' The words were cliché, inadequate. But they were the only words he had. Doctor Sinesh waved them away, shrugging in what looked like embarrassment. 'Please. It's not such a big deal. I warn you, the pain management is very likely to fail, probably in no more than a year. And it's doubtful that I – or whoever is sitting in this office at the time – will be able to repeat the trick. I've only delayed things. You will still have to have this hand replaced.'

Arnold nodded, slowly, to indicate that he absolutely understood. 'Nevertheless,' he insisted. 'Thank you so much. You've no idea how much this means to me.'

She smiled at him again. 'I think I probably do,' she suggested, and as if on some silent cue, they both stood at the same time. She opened the door, still grinning at him. 'Goodbye, doctor,' he said, and in absence of anything else to say, repeated 'thank you.'

She shook her head in a don't-mention-it gesture. 'Goodbye, Arnold Six,' she replied. She stuck out her hand, gifting him with one final, brilliant smile. 'Let me shake you by your hand. By your hand.' Arnold did, resisting the instinct to embrace her.

He walked out into the day, which seemingly in an effort to match his mood, was now a lot sunnier. On a whim, he decided to enjoy it, and walk, leaving the car where it was. He began to whistle, something he could not remember doing in well over fifty years.

He was still him.

EVERY LITTLE THING SHE DOES

And when she was done insulting him, the witch spat in his face.

Edward Locke smiled, ensuring that everyone in the room could see his smile, and slowly brushed a cuff over his chin. In fairness, his cuff was probably dirtier than the witch's spittle, but he didn't want any part of her dripping on him. She continued to stare at him, unblinking, her own chin held high. Usually at this point the querulous little bitches began to beg for their lives, screaming that they were innocent, that they had families to tend to. If Edward ever in the unlikely danger of feeling disquiet at their pleas, he would only ever need to look over at the menfolk, half shrouded in darkness. That was enough to ease any concerns: the husbands had usually passed through the mourning period in their heads already, and had their eyes on some young girl in the village who had not yet escaped their father's house.

If you were ever to catch Edward Locke in an unguarded moment and ask him if he genuinely believed that there was such a thing as witches, he would have been honestly confused by the enquiry. The work of his life, entrusted to him by the church, was to locate and eliminate all those accused of witchcraft. The devil took a gleeful and destructive turn in his attempts to overrun the country with evil, and it was the pleasant duty of noble men such as Edward Locke himself to exterminate these ungodly beings. It was therefore irrelevant to him if he had ever seen proof of witchcraft: it was more than enough that the results of dark magic had been seen, and it was his task to destroy the progenitors.

On occasion, some of the women accused of witchery would offer themselves to him. They did not know of course (or perhaps they did not care) that innocent women, pure and devoted to their husbands and to God, would never contemplate such trickery. But he enjoyed them nonetheless, delighting in their looks of confusion when he produced the pin during their carnal activities, testing their bare flesh for the proof that their body had already been procured for Old Nick.

There were other women (frustratingly, it was often the younger ones, the ones that were the most desirable of any village that Locke visited) who refused to bargain their body in exchange for freedom. They were under the sad delusion that their fellow villagers would vouch for their innocence. But once these women had the stench of accusation tainting them, most intelligent souls would ever stay silent or even provide evidence that helped prove the accused guilty.

In the cases of the women who refused him, the ones who were too stupid to offer their virtue to save themselves from eternal damnation, Locke was compelled to take that which his right by force. If they scratched or bit him, it was a simple matter to break their neck there and then. A noose or Locke's own hands, most villagers did not care how they rid themselves of a witch.

There was no need to ask Edward Locke if he enjoyed his work. It was manifestly clear that he did.

Witchcraft could be found wherever you looked. In truth, there was very little difference between one village and the next. Locke would always ensure that word was sent ahead of him, so that people were well aware of his impending arrival. (It was very pleasing that his man was called John, even if he were no Baptist, and Locke himself was certainly not Christ). Sending word ahead was not to give women enough time to flee (where would they go?) but to give the people of each village an opportunity to decide who they suspected. People would almost always find someone.

Almost. Here, in the latest village, there had been the usual shuffling and deference. He could always see when there was defiance in people's eyes, the hooded anger in people's expressions. But it was usually enough to enquire oh-so-casually exactly how long this patch of land had been in their family. That was usually enough to quell any possible uprising, and bring forth a passionate argument regarding the ungodly habits of their neighbours. Locke was nothing if not fair. But in this village, however, he had been continually frustrated. It was rare, but it did happen, on occasion: a tiny population that had somehow managed the usually difficult task of loving both God and one another. There had been no bitter feud or long burning jealousy for Locke to exploit. Neighbour looked after neighbour and they all looked at him with not fear, but something close to contempt. He had had to move swiftly to bring the village to the understanding that the childless apothecary by the river was not to be trusted when there was a god-fearing doctor readily available. It took slightly less than six hours from Locke's arrival in the village until the execution of the witch. There were a few elders who wished to protest, he could tell. But once he had shown them the seal of the king, they fell to their knees and thanked him. He let them go only once they had paid his fee.

*

He rotated his shoulders, enjoying the clicking sound it produced. He rested his hand on his belly, contemplating what he should have for supper when he gradually noticed the thin, sallow man standing in the corner of the room. Not a man, in fact: hardly a boy. John Besta was surely not even fifteen, and cursed with the sickly complexion that had always suggested to Locke that the boy would be dead long before he had any reason to shave.

'How long have you been there, boy?' Locke demanded. Besta replied that he had arrived earlier that morning. Locke realised that that meant the boy had been standing, not daring to sit or even take a piss, for over four hours while he waited for his master's arrival. Not bothering to hide his sneer, Locke dropped down onto a chair. He contemplated just ignoring Besta, just to test how well trained he really was, but decided to keep quiet for just long enough for Besta to understand that he, Locke, was not going to offer the boy a seat. And then:

'What, then?' The fact that Besta had returned to this village, and was not already at tomorrow's destination, was clearly of some importance, and he wasn't stupid enough to make a mistake: he had been too well trained.

Besta, clearly exhausted, was confused. 'Your pardon, sir?'

'You're a messenger. What is your message? Or did you come all the way back from Barrow to prop my door open?'

There was another confused moment as Besta briefly considered if the second option was indeed the correct answer, before shaking his head. 'No, sir. I have news from the court. The whole country will know it by morning.'

Locke's skin suddenly felt too tight on his skull. He leaned forward. If the entire country was to have the news by morning, then Besta was not the only messenger out today. There would be hundreds of others. Which meant that the news was vital. Which meant –

'The King,' Locke breathed.

'Is dead,' Besta provided after a short period of silence.

*

Locke did not have much time. The King's daughter – soon to be crowned Queen – had often voiced displeasure at his actions, even going as far to suggest that there was no such thing as witches. The accident of her bloodline, and the fact that she rarely left the court, had so far insulated her from reproach. Thus far, few outside the royal circle had been subjected to her inflammatory opinions. Certainly many of the lesser women in the palace had been executed for saying – even suggesting – a great deal less. But Locke had been appointed to his duties by God – and more importantly, the king himself – and so his word was sacrosanct. Locke had to move quickly, to tell the world. The future Queen, he was certain, would not let him continue in his work. He had to ensure that he was safe from her querulous, petty revenge. Yes, she would now be the Queen, but what of it? He was a man, created in God's own image. By the time he was in a carriage leaving the village, he knew what he was going to say. The woman that England was about to make its Queen had already been consumed by the devil, and he would tell the world: Queen Maria was a witch.

*

He arrived at court a little after four in the morning. He had been travelling almost continually for a little under a day, which is to say that the carriage in which he had sat had been moving almost all that time: the horses had been changed three times, and John, anticipating Locke's demands, had brought along his little brother (even smaller, even thinner) to share the riding duties. There was no bed in the carriage, but Locke had managed to doze for some of the journey. By the time he stepped out into the harsh, icy mists of London, he wasn't exactly refreshed, but he felt he could present a fair approximation to any of the king's men he had to talk to.

'My lord.' Tully appeared out of nowhere, and fell into step alongside Locke as they both approached the castle battlements. The king's closest confidante was surely comfortably into his eight decade, but looked as sprightly and alert as ever. This was infuriating: Locke had hoped to catch the household still sleeping. It was to be expected that they would all still be in mourning for the king, and bereavement often exhausts a family. In addition, they would surely want Maria to be well rested when she was crowned Queen, which if they moved fast, could happen as early as Saturday.

Locke would have to act quickly. Yes, Maria could be challenged at any time by anyone with even the most flimsy claim to the throne (it certainly helped that Maria had always been considered to be far too outspoken as a child to be ever considered truly popular – even by her own father), but such an overthrow – even if it happened within days – could take far too long to protect Locke. Even if Maria was Queen for a single day, it would give her enough time to demand his execution.

Locke decided to test the weight of his authority. 'I have a concern of which I must speak with you.' Tully stopped very suddenly, forcing Locke to halt his own pace. This was not how he wanted it to be: he was supposed to be the one controlling events. By now, they had reached the courtyard. It was not covered, but the high walls offered some protection from the elements. Flames burning on old tallow created dancing shadows on the walls. Tully did not look at him, choosing instead to stare intently at the ground just ahead of them. 'Tell me of your concern.'

Locke nodded eagerly. Tully had been the most trusted of the king's men. He would listen, and he would be persuaded. He continued to look ahead. Locke found that he was unable to resist looking the same way, and was nonplussed when he found that they were both looking at a large pile of gently steaming horse manure.

Tearing his eyes away, he looked back at Tully. 'The crown is vulnerable. The nation mourns for a great and decent king.' Tully waited patiently, saying nothing. Locke continued. 'We cannot allow her to stain the throne.' Apart from some weakly flickering torches, there was very little light in the courtyard. Even so, Locke fancied he could see Tully's eyebrow arch sharply.

'I am compelled to voice your concerns to the Queen,' Tully said, and Locke found that even though they were only a few feet from one another, he could not see any kind of expression in Tully's face at all, he was completely shrouded in darkness. It was, it suddenly occurred to him, as if the older man's head had been removed from his neck. Something about what Tully had said did not quite make sense, but he could not find the words to question it.

If Tully's expression was hidden, the same clearly was not true for Locke, because Tully now spoke to his question as yet still unvoiced. 'Our glorious Queen was crowned this morning.' Tully raised a hand, and Locke could hear footsteps approaching. 'The Bishop was in the room administering last rites, anyway, seemed a shame to make him do a return journey.' Locke could not see, but could hear, the smile in Tully's voice. The footsteps stopped. Hands gripped both of Locke's arms. Tully finally stepped out of the shadows. 'Please come this way. Her majesty is very keen to speak with you.'

*

The crowd was very excited, full of fevered mutterings. The Witchfinder had been commanded to stand, but otherwise he was quite unable to move far: the chains held him directly to the straw covered floor. He had no tongue with which to make a complaint about his current situation for the very simple reason that he no longer had a tongue. It had been torn from his mouth with very little fuss or ceremony earlier in the day. The action had caused much distress to the Witchfinder, and much joy for the dog that was often to be found begging for scraps at the castle kitchen. The dog considered itself well fed tonight.

The Queen strode into the Great Hall, hardly noticing as each head bowed to her. 'Edward Locke,' she said in a voice that carried well and filled the hall, 'You claim to be doing God's work. You have murdered my sisters – because understand me, each woman in England is my sister.' She paused for a moment, and looked around her. She wanted to ensure the court fully understood her words. When she was certain she had everyone's attention, she began to walk once more.

'No doubt you have men in your employ who still fear me and fear the women in their own houses, who will seek to kill me – the Queen – because they misapprehend They might dare to exact revenge on my sisters. They believe England's throne is befouled by a witch.' She said all of this as she walked, not stopping to break her pace. Now, she was standing in front of Locke, and she leaned into his ear. He couldn't see her clearly, but he could tell by the touch of her lips that she was smiling. 'They believe all this without proof. I think it correct we should give them proof.'

The Queen stepped away from Locke, and strode up to her throne. She smiled. The smile became a laugh. Dutifully, the court laughed also. Locke didn't make any sound at all. The Queen flickered a glance at a pillar just behind Locke. If the court did not have their heads bowed, they might have seen a shadow move. 'After all,' the Queen continued softly, 'it seems only fair to let you know what you're up against.' She dropped her hand. Within moments, the entire court was screaming.

*

Historical documents have failed to reach a consensus about what happened next. One of the more colourful accounts would have readers believe that Locke exploded where he stood, but most historians are satisfied with the slightly more prosaic – but no less surprising – explanation that he simply burst into flames. His chains held him still firmly in place as he struggled for his freedom, and his ragged tongue meant that he was never able to call out for rescue or mercy, but it was agreed by all present that day that even a man who possesses no tongue will still somehow be able to scream in agony. It took Locke nearly ninety minutes to die, by which time there was nobody in the court who doubted the Queen's power. The only other thing that all accounts agree on was that the sun shone brightly on Edward Locke's corpse.

The Queen addressed her court in what would prove to be her shortest address of her lengthy reign. She stated her hope that her subjects understood her power, and further, that they appreciated that any one of her sisters were capable of wielding the same power if pushed. Queen Maria invited her court to speak freely. Eventually, one man approached her, then lay face down on the ground. 'Long live the Queen,' he declared.

The court repeated the chant. 'Long live the Queen!' Maria smiled, and breathed in deep. The smell of charred flesh lingered for days.

*

As soon as he heard her footsteps in his little workshop, Pox leapt to his feet, and bowed low. 'Please forgive me if I do not take your hand, my lady,' he said, seeing that she had offered hers. 'My own are still covered in tallow,' he explained.

She nodded, satisfied. 'The deception will succeed, you think?'

Pox grinned shyly, not quite allowing himself to be in any way familiar with his Queen. 'You had their respect before. This casts it in iron.'

'And my subjects? Each woman knows that she is my sister?'

'If they do not today, they will by the end of the night.'

She nodded again.

'We thank you for your service.'

Pox bowed.

*

A chicken clucked irritably at the old woman, reminding her that this was not her land. She pushed the fear to the back of her belly, and pushed herself on. She only had to turn one corner before she found Susannah, already slicked with grime and sweat at this early hour. Her eyes widened. 'Mother!' she cried, in both surprise and admonishment. 'You best get out of here before the master sees you!'

Martha set her jaw. Wentworth might be the farmer here, but he was not Susannah's master, no matter what he had done to her in the last six weeks since his wife had been executed by the Witchfinder who had passed through. Susannah was just a naïve little girl, and deserved nothing other than to be back with the family who loved her. 'I'm here to take you home,' she told her daughter, surprised at how strong her voice sounded. Susannah's eyes widened even further. 'You should go. He'll hurt you.' Martha did not answer right away; she had already seen the cut healing below her daughter's eye. 'Put your things down,' she said at last. 'You'll not do a moment for him no more.'

The door of the farmhouse swung open, and Wentworth emerged, stopping as soon as he saw Martha. His hand dropped instinctively to the knife he kept at his belt. Martha watched warily. She had seen that knife slit the neck of many a pig. 'You best be gone, old woman,' Wentworth called out, and Martha was gratified to see him lick dry lips before he spoke. 'Yes, I'll go. And I'll take my girl with me. Unless you want every sister in the village on your land?'

Wentworth was successful at delivering a derisive laugh, but did not quite trust himself to speak. Instead, he simply grabbed Susannah roughly by the arm, and pulled her toward the house. 'Get inside now, girl, or it'll be the worse for you,' Susannah's eyes fluttered up at her mother's, and a moment's eye contact was all that they needed. She pulled back her arm, and the movement was so unexpected that Wentworth let her go. 'I'll not come back to you today, Mr Wentworth,' she said, and before he could offer up an argument, she advised 'Your wife still speaks to me, you know. She is most displeased.' All three of them looked at the still charred patch of land at the side of Wentworth's house: Locke had not gone far to carry out his duties. Wentworth swallowed hard, and began to speak, when Susannah simply raised her hand. Wentworth stumbled back, and fell on the ground.

The two women watched him kindly. They did not laugh. Susannah joined her mother at the gate. 'Do you have a message for our sisters, Mr Wentworth?' asked Martha. Wentworth thought about it very carefully before answering. He got to his feet and approached them. They waited patiently. Finally, he spoke. 'Long live the Queen,' he said.

The women nodded. Wentworth's answer was satisfactory. They linked arms, and walked back into the village, where their sisters were waiting for them.

COMING SOON FROM ANDREW ALLEN

TRAVERS AND WELLS: THE CITY OF DR MOREAU (a novella)
THE HAUNTING OF GABRIEL CHASE (a novel)
IN THE MIDDLE OF THE NIGHT (stories)
THE MEMORY CHEATS (a novel)

Follow Andrew's blog on thisisandrewallen.wordpress.com
Follow Andrew on twitter/insta via @my_grayne

Printed in Great Britain
by Amazon